Praise for You Have Time for This:

"These contenders for the title of 'world's best short-short stories' are by some of the best micro and flash writers I know of, writers such as Katherine Weber, Bruce Holland Rogers, Sherrie Flick, Deb Olin Unferth, Bruce Boston, and Aimee Bender. How can they do it in less than five hundred words—suspense, revelation, a twist of metaphor or plot or character, and sometimes all—before you can turn the page? It's like levitation—I'm skeptical, but seeing is believing. A good book by two editors who are excellent flash fiction writers themselves."

Robert Shapard
Co-editor of *New Sudden Fiction* and *Flash Fiction Forward*

"You Have Time For This is a run of fifty-four epiphanies, narrative poetic diamonds. It's the kind of book you can carry around with you, nudge a friend, and say, 'Hey, listen to this!' It's a textbook in conciseness and precision, a kind of litmus against your own self indulgence. It's also a great teaching tool. Over the years Tom Hazuka has become the master of writing and mining these gems. What a pleasure."

Chuck Rosenthal
Author of *The Loop Trilogy*

"A really good flash fiction is like a story overheard at a bar—personal, funny, dangerous, and sometimes hard-to-believe. *You Have Time For This* distills those qualities and many others into quick tall tales by writers who

Pu

"These stories are like snapshots that suddenly morph into short films. Some are sober, others surreal, but all share an emotional impact that is all the more impressive in light of their length. They look you in the eye, shake your hand firmly, and whisper something nice in your ear before punching your stomach just hard enough to make you remember them."

Wyn Cooper
Author of *Postcards from the Interior*

You Have Time for This

You Have Time for This

*Contemporary American
Short-Short Stories*

edited by Mark Budman & Tom Hazuka

Ooligan Press   Portland, Oregon

You Have Time for This
Contemporary American Short-Short Stories

ISBN13: 978-1-932010-17-6

Cover design by Mike Hirte and Terra Chapek
Cover photograph by Casey Rae Wickum
All interior photographs by Casey Rae Wickum
Text set in Adobe Garamond Pro and Optima LT Std

Library of Congress Cataloging-in-Publication information available
from publisher.

Ooligan Press ■ Portland State University
P.O. Box 751, Portland, OR 97207-0751
ooligan@pdx.edu ■ www.ooliganpress.pdx.edu

10 9 8 7 6 5 4 3 2 1

Printed in the United States by Malloy Incorporated.

 Portland State
UNIVERSITY

Words must be weighed
and not counted.

Table of Contents

Introduction

Dear Reader,

What is flash fiction? In his *Hamlet*, William Shakespeare writes that "Brevity is the soul of wit." Brevity. What a word pregnant with meaning! Yet brevity alone cannot be the answer; otherwise "I want food" or "Give me money" would be excellent examples of flash fiction.

Flash fiction rests on a tripod of plot, language, and characters. And yes, it has to be brief. Think tabletop tripod and not the one a large telescope sits on. How brief? For purposes of this book, 500 words or less. At this short length, the tripod has to be precise and the focus right on target. No wobbling, no mincing of words. Remove one leg of the tripod, and the story will collapse, the publisher will turn away, or the reader will leave yawning. That's the worst punishment for a writer.

Writing a memorable story in only 500 words is a challenge. We encourage you to practice, and to try to write flash fiction yourself. Like a sculptor with a block of stone, you must cut unnecessary words until you get to the very core of the story and your senses tell you that you can't cut any more. Yet at the same time, nothing important can be left out.

Rich, literary fiction can never be completely understood, by writer, by editor, or by reader. Various possible interpretations are always possible. That's why authors need intelligent readers to cooperate in the process of making sense of a text.

What should you pay attention to when you read flash fiction? First, appreciate the author's ability to squeeze the essence of a situation into such a tight form. Notice the intricacy of language that is poetic yet also tells a story. Pay careful attention to every word, as if you were reading a poem, because in good flash fiction every word is important.

Finally, flash fiction is ideally suited for today's world of instant gratification. Anyone has time to read a one- or two-page story. When it is well crafted and firm upon the flash fiction tripod, it satisfies innate cravings for the fine word, memorable characters, and the twist of plot, and it works its magic in a flash.

Mark Budman

SLEEPING

She would not have to change a diaper, they said. In fact, she would not have to do anything at all. Mrs. Winter said that Charles would not wake while she and Mr. Winter were out at the movies. He was a very sound sleeper, she said. No need to have a bottle for him or anything. Before the Winters left they said absolutely please not to look in on the sleeping baby because the door squeaked too loudly.

Harriet had never held a baby, except for one brief moment, when she was about six, when Mrs. Antler next door had surprisingly bestowed on her the tight little bundle that was their new baby, Andrea. Harriet had sat very still and her arms had begun to ache from the tension by the time Mrs. Antler took back her baby. Andy was now a plump seven-year-old, older than Harriet had been when she held her that day.

After two hours of reading all of the boring mail piled neatly on a desk in the bedroom and looking through a depressing wedding album filled with photographs of dressed-up people in desperate need of orthodonture (Harriet had just ended two years in braces and was very conscious of malocclusion issues) while flipping channels on their television, Harriet turned the knob on the baby's door very tentatively, but it seemed locked. She didn't dare turn the knob with more pressure because what if she made a noise and woke him and he started to cry?

She stood outside the door and tried to hear the sound of a baby breathing but she couldn't hear anything through the door but the sound of the occasional car that passed by on the street outside. She wondered what Charles looked like. She wasn't even sure how old he was. Why had she agreed to baby-sit when Mr. Winter approached her at the swim club? She had never seen him before, and it was flattering that he took her for being capable, as if just being a girl her age automatically qualified her as a baby-sitter.

By the time the Winters came home, Harriet had eaten most of the M&M'S® in the glass bowl on their coffee table: first all the blue ones, then the red ones, then all the green ones, and so on, leaving, in the end, only the yellow.

They gave her too much money and didn't ask her about anything. Mrs. Winter seemed to be waiting for her to leave before checking on the baby. Mr. Winter drove her home in silence. When they reached her house he said, My wife. He hesitated, then he said, You understand, don't you? and Harriet answered Yes without looking at him or being sure what they were talking about although she did really know what he was telling her and then she got out of his car and watched him drive away.

Katharine Weber is the author of the novels Objects in the Mirror Are Closer Than They Appear (Crown, 1995), The Music Lesson (Crown, 1999), The Little Women (Farrar, Straus & Giroux, 2003), and Triangle (Farrar, Straus & Giroux, 2006). Her short stories have appeared in the New Yorker, Story, Redbook, Gargoyle, the Readerville Journal, and Southwest Review. Katharine has taught fiction writing at Connecticut College, Yale University, and the Paris Writers Workshop. She was the Kratz Writer in Residence at Goucher College in Spring 2006. Visit her at http://www.katharineweber.com/.

Steve Almond

REUNIFICATION

In East Berlin, some years ago, after the wall and fresh into the era of bistros, copper fixtures and fatty salads, an acquaintance, a pretty American, perhaps not as pretty as she took herself to be, a young student of Germans and Jews, supporting herself on grant money and dressed in silk, beset by her ideas and red wine, announced to me that all art is political.

How can art live apart from the culture? she said, and all I could think was that fucking her might be the disastrous material I needed; she seemed far from understanding anything. We had that in common. Or maybe that's where I wanted to be, in her doubtless quadrant, shouting the truth onto its knees and borrowing from history a crude form of self-belief.

I was failing in my own art, after all, unmoored from America, tumbling through the world as if it were the set of a cheap romance.

So I sat at dinner in the new East and nodded at her citations (Riefenstahl, Guernica) as a flirt, but quickly tired of her voice. She wouldn't let it go, though, kept on and on, hard, until we reached the metro where, in the camphorous light, in the glowing things of civilization all around us, a single silkworm rappelled delicately from the ticket kiosk.

How can we know to what end our creation will be put? How can we care? I should have punched her in the nose for saying such a thing. But I wanted to sleep with her.

I am just as rich in foolish lusts these days. And I spin only because I would fall if I didn't.

Steve Almond is the author of the story collections The Evil B.B. Chow and My Life in Heavy Metal, as well as the nonfiction book Candyfreak and the epistolary novel Which Brings Me to You, co-written with Julianna Baggott. He spent seven years as a newspaper reporter, mostly in El Paso and Miami, and has been writing fiction for the last eight years. His work has been published in many literary magazines. He lives outside of Boston, and can be found online at http://www. stevenalmond.com.

THE DEAD

We walk every morning, our pace well suited—old dog and old woman—a leash uniting us in silent journeys down country roads. The redwoods and Douglas firs creak in winter gusts that push us along. The sky is a changing panorama of purest pinks and the clear blues of newborns' eyes. Glorious enough to explain why people think heaven is skyward. The mist steams on a horizon of pines.

A dead mouse in the road is tiny, scrawny, with gray fur. If not for the black ooze beneath its head, it looks asleep. I drag Murphy away, his nose urged toward the scent.

The following morning, we see a thin snake flattened on the pavement, its scales glittery in the early light. Its skin is unharmed, like a flower pressed under the wheels of a car or truck. As I again yank Murphy from the kill, I see movement—an infant is silhouetted, perched high in a tall, soft fir. It's a flash, an image. I cup my hand over my eyes, but she is gone—a mirage.

Next outing, bitter cold, the trudge up Arcadia Road is arduous. Murphy's fur ripples against his flanks in the wind. I wonder, for the millionth time, how different life might be, had the child been born. I shiver with cold and my dark thoughts.

"Better take a quick whiz, Murph," I say. The wind shakes the trees, making a whooshing eerie rustle. The dawn skies are flat and gray.

On the road an injured wren huddles, motionless. I hold Murphy back as I swoop it up. It struggles only a little. I move it gently to the grassy shoulder where it sits, immobile, while my mind battles between leaving it to survive in nature, or taking it home. Murphy's interest has been captured by a movement in the trees.

The baby appears again in the fir. No mistake. She is perched naked and rosy on an outer limb. The tight curls of her hair are honey-colored, and her face dimples with mirth as she waves her tiny fist.

It begins in my chest, and explodes in my ears, filling my mouth and nose. My head rings with the screech of wind and cries that must be born in my own constricted throat.

For years I've wondered what she'd look like, this child of mine. She gaily waves and I lift my hand in response, as if our fluttering fingers spin a thread, forever connecting us. She waits, I now know.

The vision of her fades in and out of the dappled foliage of the woods.

At my feet, the bird takes a few faltering steps, and I swipe my wet face with the sleeve of my parka. When I look back, the empty branches, heavy with needles, sway, waving.

The wren lifts off in a dazed and haphazard little circle. Then, buoyed by wind, it soars up into the trees.

Beverly A. Jackson is a writer of poetry and short fiction, and former editor and publisher of Ink Pot and Lit Pot Press, Inc. Her work has appeared in both print and online literary journals including Vestal Review, Melic Review, Night Train, Zoetrope All-Story Extra, Absinthe Review, God Particle, and Rattle, to name only a few. She is working on her first novel, titled The Loose Fish Chronicles. You can find her online at http://www.beverlyajackson.com.

Deb Olin Unferth

MAYBE A SUPERHERO

She had an affair, not because she didn't love her husband or because he was unkind or uninteresting, but because she was transforming into a machine sort of thing or maybe a superhero. A soft alloy built inside her. Her heart shifted from a thump to a tick-tock. She padded barefoot through the house, left a thin trail of shavings behind her. She could shoot metal pellets a great distance with a nozzle that protruded from her belly button.

Her husband found her unfit for their current lifestyle. "Don't touch me," he said. Beneath the polish, her nails were steel. "No more spas in Mexico," he said. "You're unseemly in a bikini."

She suspected her transformation may be immoral or evil. She worked hard to conceal it, slid the nozzle in as far as it would go. At dinner she kept her eyes still and focused. He hated to hear the click of the shutter, the buzz of the zoom.

In aisle eight, hardware, she met another man in the same condition. He stole a screwdriver, pushed it through his ear with a snap. It was natural they would bond. He was a little wild, less intelligent than her husband. He rode with the windows down no matter the weather. He wore torn shirts, rubbed ashes from his cigarettes into his jeans. He was an airplane mechanic and his heart was shifting from a pulse to a whir. Inside his arms, blood flowed through aluminum tubes. The two lovers raced like engines at each other in his pick-up. She oiled between her legs.

She now came with directions: Insert two fingers and turn left until loose. They screwed on a table at his place. He shouted, "Have my baby!" Neither of them wanted that thrust to pull. She arched her back. "Shoot it in."

She had his baby! But she didn't give up her husband. She had both of their babies and flew back and forth between planets. She grew a propeller from her head. They were cute, the men, with their hedge clippers and robes. They waved hello as she landed on the sidewalk. But she couldn't very well show up on the other planet with the wrong baby on her back. She had to leave the babies behind with the men.

But her husbands soon wanted divorces. "Who wants you?" one said. "You're flying around all the time." "What sort of mother," the other said, "goes off and leaves her baby at home?"

The settlement papers came through on a Friday. She sat on the swing set in the rain. Why worry about rust? She had done it, she had tried. She was the best mom and wife in both worlds, man and machine. She had room for them all—men, babies and she could fit more!—in her little metal heart.

Deb Olin Unferth's fiction has appeared or is forthcoming in Harper's, NOON, Fence, 3rd bed, StoryQuarterly, the Denver Quarterly, and other journals. She received a Pushcart Prize and a fellowship from the Illinois Arts Council. She is a founder and editor of Parakeet.

CLAWD

My old man brought home a gift from Texas or Arizona. It beat the customary stick of Wrigley's Spearmint from his suit coat pocket. It was live. It was a praying mantis.

I named it Clawd. I watched him for hours. His spiky caliper arms swayed at guard like a sparring boxer. Behind them, his head gyrated, incessantly seeking prey. In tender moments his claws would snap onto my fingertip.

Unlike other insect pets, Clawd ate heartily. His favorite meal was grasshopper. Fine with me, coming home from school most days with grasshopper tobacco juice on my fingers.

Clawd would freeze curious with the grasshopper I'd caught. Then, *fwat*, he'd grab it at the top of the thorax and in the middle of the abdomen. His little mouth would gouge great chunks from the back, chomping away like me with corn on the cob. The grasshopper would struggle with half its back gone in an open brown wound.

Clawd lived in a sturdy shoebox in the basement. For his view and ventilation, I cut out parts of the box and replaced them with screen. For his exercise, I caught flies and let him flail away at them.

One day in late summer, Clawd refused to move. I nudged his arms and his whole body was stiff like a twig. I dropped to my knees for a closer look. His abdomen was flat as a small elm leaf. I moved some of the dead grass and saw an oval gray blob. Clawd had died from shitting his guts out.

I buried him in a velvet jeweler's box with a satin interior. I tied a cross with twine and two sticks. I stuck it in the ground where the lawn mower couldn't reach. His cage with the blob was chucked into the trash.

Years later I read a text with the facts of life for praying mantises. The female eats her mate during or just after making love. Months later the female lays the egg pod and dies. I stared at the close-up photo of the egg pod. It looked familiar. I should have named Clawd Clawdette.

I find solace knowing that in a dump warmed by the city's decomposing garbage, thousands of Clawdette's descendants roam free, hundreds of miles from their natural habitat. Eating a cornucopia of bugs. Breeding and dying with smiles on their faces, their arms clutched in eternal prayer.

G. W. Cox spent twenty-six years in newspaper work. He now lives and writes in New Mexico with his wife, Magda, and their pet dog.

David Schuman

Indian Casino

My son wakes me in the middle of the night. This is unusual because he is a heavy sleeper—he once slept through a hailstorm that left pockmarks on the hood of the car and two crushed robins in the backyard.

"We need to go to the casino," he says. "I had a dream."

I mumble something about it being two-thirty in the morning but he is unimpressed.

"Mom was in the dream," he says, and hands me my pants.

His mother, my wife, has been dead for a year and three months.

The river takes an hour to get to, and there's the casino, garish against a dingy dawn sky. Beyond the flashing lights, a barge glides past on the river. I have read about pleasure boats that get too close to the barges, underestimating their speed. It is all over for them.

"She said you had to play the slots. She was sort of singing it," he says, pressing silver dollars into my hand, one by one, until there's a little column of them in my palm.

"This isn't tooth fairy money?" I ask. The look that he gives me could remove paint from a wall.

"Say her name when you pull the lever," he says.

I leave him three stories up in the garage, parked behind a pillar of concrete as thick as a redwood. I tell him to keep the doors locked, against who I'm not sure, but a casino parking lot is no place for a boy. A few days before she died, I saw my wife push my son's hair out of his eyes as he lay with her in the hospital bed. "Be good, little onion," she said. I order his favorite pepperoni pizzas instead of making meatloaf and vegetables, I take him to science fiction movies that his friends' parents won't let them see, and I bought him a parakeet who shits on my shoulders, but "little onion" is the thing he is going to remember as long as he lives.

There are more people in the casino than I thought would be here this early. The carpet has a pattern of tomahawks, but I don't think Indians have anything to do with this place. The gamblers carry jumbo plastic soda cups with tokens inside.

You expect me to say that I came out of there with nothing, but that is not what happened. When I open the car door, my son is roused from sleep. The pattern from the upholstery is impressed on his cheek.

"Did we get lucky?" he says.

For the first time I have something to tell him.

David Schuman teaches fiction writing at Washington University in St. Louis, Missouri, where he is also assistant director of the graduate writing program. His fiction has been published in numerous literary journals, including Conjunctions, Missouri Review, and Black Warrior Review. He is the executive editor of Land-Grant College Review, a literary magazine based in New York City.

Chauna Craig

THE MAN WITH THE SHOVEL

The man with the shovel dreamed once of the trapeze. He was a boy then. He'd gone to the circus with his father, a man who would leave. The air flashed bright with red leotards, bodies flipping through space. Someone always caught these bodies with slender hands, slight fingers that could miss or snap off like twigs. But first came the breathless moment, the what if.

What did you like best?

The man who would leave was still there then, driving fast in the dark as the boy slumped under his seatbelt. His stomach cramped with cotton candy and warm lemonade. The seatbelt pinched and pulled. He said, the flying people.

You mean the acrobats? People can't fly.

And he nodded, yes, the acrobats who lived on air.

The man with the shovel is too slow for the one who drives the orange public works truck. He moves slower as the day grows long. The driver honks and swears. *They're fuckin' animals. They're fuckin' dead. They don't need last rites.*

The man with the shovel never explains. He scrapes the squirrels from suburban drives, gently balancing them as he steps towards the truck. He knows they've been hit by things they couldn't outrun. Some are flattened, bloody pelts.

But so many of the bodies he lifts are soft and whole. He pretends their toes missed a branch, that a tiny twig gave. Maybe their hearts burst from the altitude. Yes, he thinks when he sees no blood, burst hearts.

He launches them from the end of his shovel. They flip in the air, white bellies flashing through sunlight. Flying squirrels. *People can't fly.* Squirrels limp as those acrobat bodies in the moments before they were caught. Late in the day, when the truck bed is full, lined with feathers and fur and the odors of decay, he knows they land safe.

The man with the shovel dreamed once of the trapeze. He was a boy then. When the driver backs in and raises the end, broken bodies slide into the pit that yawns like a mouth. Fur and feathers collapse. Squirrels and birds and the cats that chased them, nestled now in eternal truce.

The man with the shovel waits near the piled earth. All is still, except the delirious flies. All is muted and dirt-dulled but the guts. They shine red, bright leotards stripped inside out.

Chauna Craig is a professor of creative writing at Indiana University of Pennsylvania. Her stories have appeared in numerous literary magazines and anthologies, including Sudden Stories: A Mammoth Anthology of Miniscule Fiction. Her work has also been cited in Best American Essays and the Pushcart Prize anthology.

The way to love anything is to
realize that it might be lost.

Randall DeVallance

Parting Ways

There was the death, of course, and the funeral and a week later, Marianne visited the grave for the first time. She took along a small bouquet of roses, white ones, and laid them on the grass in front of the headstone. Knowing she needed this time alone, I waited by the car and smoked a cigarette. I fully admit that I was indifferent to her plight, but I had no desire to upset her further, and so kept myself at a distance where I would not have to become involved.

The person who died I did not know. But to Marianne it was someone important, which I guess made her important to me. It was sunny and cold, and a breeze made Marianne's long, blonde hair swirl and dance like the clouds of smoke I pushed from my lips. It was the only thing distinguishing her from one of the monuments: she stood perfectly erect, head bowed, hands clasped in front of her waist. Dressed all in black—the heels and the stockings, the peacoat and beret—she seemed only more pale.

An hour passed that way, but I was not impatient with her. The cemetery was not unappealing to me: aesthetically, I had the deepest appreciation for it. The exactness of the monuments, the obvious care that went into their making, from the grandest mausoleum to the most modest grave marker, spoke of a sincerity that had seemingly disappeared from our lives. It had retreated here, to a place where cynicism could never intrude, where the source of all our dread and bitter joys was memorialized, spreading out beyond the edge of sight, in every direction, to a place my eyes could not reach.

When the sun had fallen lower, filtered gold through the boughs of the oak trees that dotted the grounds, I summoned the courage to speak Marianne's name. But she made no answer, and I could see then that she was already too far gone, that no matter what I said or how I pleaded, she was simply not ready to leave. Perhaps she would never be ready. Coming up behind her, I leaned in and kissed her one last time on the cheek. Her eyes remained fixed on the headstone as I got in the car and drove away, leaving her to recede in the rearview mirror.

Randall DeVallance is a 2002 graduate of Edinboro University. More than twenty of his short stories have appeared in such publications as Eyeshot, Opium Magazine, Vestal Review, and Pindeldyboz. He has earned a Pushcart nomination and a place on StorySouth's Notable Stories of 2004 list. His first novel, Dive, was published in 2004 by Exquisite Cadaver Press. He is currently serving with the Peace Corps in Zemen, Bulgaria.

THE STORY OF YOU

You were lean and dark-haired in your open-air Jeep. You made your left turn and I followed, all the way to the café on South Beverly Drive. I took a corner table, drank a mocha latte, watched you flirt with the redhead. Guys came up, asked for a seat and a chance. I licked foam off my lips. I only wanted you.

Weeks passed, and I learned you so well. You approached me in the club, said, "How come we don't know each other?" We squeezed onto the dance floor. I put my mouth to the warm salty hollow between neck and shoulder, moved my tongue along your skin until I found your pulse.

That was my first taste of you.

You never learned me at all. "She's a sweet girl," I heard you say on the phone. "She would never do anything like that." That was your version, which begins We met at a club, and ends, I'm in love with Lucinda. I'm sorry. I hope we'll be friends.

But it began at the corner of Wilshire and Beverly Glen, your wild swing into a reckless left.

The heft of the gun in my purse. The way to your house through this maze of sun-slammed streets.

I am the one telling the story, my love.

I will be your ending.

Justine Musk was born in 1972 in a small town in Ontario, Canada. She went to Queen's University and graduated with a first-class degree in English literature. After living and working in Australia and Japan, she moved to California. She is the author of three dark-fantasy novels, Bloodangel (Roc/Penguin), Slayer of Angels (Roc/Penguin), and Stranger (MTV Books/Simon & Schuster), which will be published in 2007. She lives in Los Angeles with her husband, young sons, and dogs.

Mark Budman

THE DARK SIDE OF THE MOON

When I was six, I waded into the Black Sea until the water reached my cute belly button. I asked my father, "What's on other side?"

"Bulgaria," he said. That sounded dry, like an arid bagel.

"And after that?"

"Western Europe."

I knew what a Western was—a movie where they ride horses and fight Indians.

"And after that?"

"The Atlantic Ocean."

"And behind the ocean?"

"America."

I knew Americans wore top hats, smoked cigars, exploited workers and wanted to bomb everybody, especially my Motherland. But I didn't know they were that far.

"What is closer, America or the moon?"

"Spanking," my dad said with his usual half-smile. "That's the closest thing to you." He thought for a second and added, "Violence determines conciseness."

I didn't know he was making a Russian-language pun on the Marxist maxim "Environment determines conciseness."

Many years later, I stood at the New Jersey shore and watched clouds eat the pale moon by the Eastern horizon. The cell phone rang.

"It'd better be good," I said.

"It's done, boss," was the reply.

I hung up and stuck my cigar back into my mouth. If you blow the whistle in my company, you won't last long.

Mark Budman has always been interested in short-shorts. To him, a short-short is not only a stepping stone to writing longer fiction, but a drawing power that could bring the busy masses back to literature. With his co-editor Sue O'Neill, he started Vestal Review, a magazine of flash fiction, back in March of 2000. Together with Sue, he has published thirty quarterly issues so far. Mark has been lecturing widely on the subject of flash. He taught it at Binghamton University, Ithaca College, Broome Community College, Art School Online, and he is scheduled to be a panelist for the Saltonstall Foundation. Mark was born and raised in the former Soviet Union, but now resides in New York state. His novel My Life at First Try was scheduled for publication in May of 2008 by Counterpoint.

HOMEWARD BOUND

Thanksgiving, 1970, changing planes at a Midwestern airport. I wasn't feeling thankful, not even for my sky-high draft lottery number. I felt more guilty than good about luck shielding me from decisions I'd never wish on anybody: Canada, prison, Vietnam.

A soldier in a wheelchair was smoking Luckies like his life depended on it. He had a newspaper on his lap but wasn't reading it; I saw ashes on the headlines. After a while two soldiers sat in front of me, discussing the football game. One hoped the storm would hold off because he hated god-damn turbulence.

A guy and a girl my age—college—came up to the wheelchair. "Vietnam?" he asked.

The soldier nodded.

"Good," she said. "Paralyzed, babyburner? Still got your manhood?"

"Yeah," he said, too quick, so quick it made you wonder.

The bigger soldier jumped up, but the skinny one shoved him aside. He dropped the guy with one punch, then smacked the girl twice in the face.

A black security guard my father's age ran over. "Did you *see* that?" the girl shrieked.

"I saw it." He yanked the guy to his feet. "Now *get* outta here."

His voice was so venomous they fled without speaking. The wheelchair soldier was shaking, pretending to read the paper. The other two sat down again, careful, like they weren't sure the seats fit any more.

"Sorry, man," said the skinny one, his voice full of holes. "I was afraid you couldn't do it."

I remembered going to Niagara Falls as a kid, the disappointment of crossing into Canada and not feeling any different on foreign soil. It was like the world was just all one place.

We took off late in the snowstorm.

Tom Hazuka is a professor of English at Central Connecticut State University. He has published two novels, The Road to the Island and In the City of the Disappeared, and one book of nonfiction, A Method to March Madness: An Insider's Look at the Final Four (co-written with C.J. Jones). His young adult novel, Last Chance for First, will be published in 2008. He has co-edited three other short story anthologies: A Celestial Omnibus: Short Fiction on Faith (Beacon Press); Flash Fiction (W.W. Norton); and Best American Flash Fiction of the 21st Century (Shanghai Foreign Language Education Press). His short fiction, essays, and poems have appeared in many literary magazines.

L. E. Leone

The Argument for a Shotgun

You wake up in the middle of the night afraid of what? For me it's dead chickens, no more eggs and a bloodless bloody mess to clean. Weasels'll wipe out a whole houseload of chickens in one night, only knocking off the heads and sucking out the brains. For example.

For example I dream a fox with wirecutters and a crowbar.

"Where are you going?" asks my wife.

"Bathroom," I say.

"Why are you putting on your hat? Why are you putting on your shoes?"

"Go back to sleep," I say.

In the bathroom I open the window and stick my head all the way out into northern California, middle of the night. I think I hear a scratching sound coming from the vicinity of the chicken house. Bobcat, I think, trying to dig its way under the fence.

I need a shotgun. I really should have a shotgun, I think, running outside to meet the enemy with a curling iron and a toilet-bowl brush.

The enemy, this time, is fog, condensing into water droplets on oak tree leaves and dripping onto other oak tree leaves, dripping down all the way eventually into the dead, crispy stuff I never rake around the chicken run. I stand there under the tree in the dark until my eyes adjust to no bobcats, no foxes, no hungry eyes or glistening teeth; just fog, just watery particles of atmosphere, the is of what isn't, suspended like berries all around me—visible only because up there somewhere there's a moon.

I stand where I am until my heartrate returns to normal. Then I brandish the toilet-bowl brush, stab at the fog with the curling iron, and head back inside.

"What was it?" my wife asks.

"Nothing," I say.

L. E. (Dan) Leone writes a weekly humorous column about food and life for the San Francisco Bay Guardian. L. E. has published two books, The Meaning of Lunch (Mammoth Press, 2000), and Eat This, San Francisco (Sasquatch Books, 2002), as well as numerous stories in literary magazines and anthologies.

Damn Irene

Harry dipped his paddle blade, the handle at chest level as Toni the Leader had taught them. Just beyond the three kayaks crouched a damp roll of fog; if he reached out, he could've grabbed a handful.

"We'll make for Burnt Island," Toni called. "It's getting murky—stick together, we won't get lost."

"Okay," Harry shouted. In the rear seat, Irene said nothing. He glanced back; she paddled clumsily, her face expressionless above her life vest. A wave tossed up spray. He shivered. Cold; he'd hate to have to swim in this bay.

"Left," Toni called. "Follow me."

Harry leaned into the paddle, dipping, dipping, but the kayak did not turn. Fog tickled his arm. "Left, Irene," he ordered. "Push the left pedal."

Behind him, her meek voice: "I can't, Honey. It's stuck. The rudder won't go left."

"You're not trying," he said through clenched teeth. Damn Irene. She never tried. She'd seemed so eager to please last year when they were dating. Then he'd married her. What a mistake.

She never complained, per se. But when he tried to teach her tennis—coached her, drilled, cajoled, rewarded, bullied, shamed her—she refused to hit the ball right. At last, he joined a club and left her to putter in her silly garden.

He bought her a bike. She didn't bother to keep up with him, and still she strained her knee.

Golf? She lost the balls. Camping? She got poison ivy. And when he took her hunting, she tripped and nearly shot him ("Oops; sorry, honey," she'd said).

Ron and Marcie's kayak shimmered off to the left and dissolved in the mist. Marcie, now—*there* was a game woman. Damn Irene. "Push your left pedal. *Push.*"

"I am, Honey."

His neck hairs bristled. "You're not."

"I told you, the right pedal works—"

He heard the rustle of the spray skirt that stretched from her waist to the rim of her compartment; the kayak lumbered rightward.

"—but not the left."

"Irene, straighten us out," he commanded.

"I can't, Honey. Honest. My left pedal's broke."

Her wimpy tone set his teeth on edge. "Damn, Irene." He twisted, heard the dip-dip of her paddle, but she was lost in fog. "Turn this kayak left. *Now.*"

Silence.

Then, softly, tentatively: "Turn it yourself." Dip-dip. "Honey."

His eyes widened. Far away, a buoy gonged.

He slammed the paddle down on the fiberglass hull. "What'd you say?" His heart hammered. He jutted his jaw. "*What??* I'll be damned if I'll paddle for two."

"This wasn't my idea." Her disembodied voice sounded surprised: "You know, it's never my idea."

He heard the snap of a spray skirt pulling free. A splash. A gasp—*Whoo!* The kayak bucked, rolled over; grey water grabbed up for him. Cold. He heard arm-strokes, surprisingly strong, receding, fading, gone. His face bobbed under, up; his paddle knocked the hull, dodged his shivering fingers, floated away.

"Damn, Irene!" Up; under. *"Ireeeb?!?"*

But there was only the far-off gong of the buoy.

Susan O'Neill writes fiction and nonfiction, has been nominated twice for the Pushcart Prize, and has been named a notable author by Best American Essays. Her book, Don't Mean Nothing: Short Stories of Vietnam (Ballantine, 2001; Black Swan [UK], 2002; and UMass Press, 2004), was based on her year as an Army nurse during the Vietnam war. She lives in Massachusetts with her husband. Visit her online at http://www.susanoneill.us.

Black Silk

We lasted ten minutes at the restaurant. Silver earrings. Alcove. Her hand on me under the table. The crushed strawberries did it, juice running down that luscious throat. She started undressing in the car, her dark skin luminous. She drew off her black silk stockings and flicked them. She kept her legs open, showing herself off to me.

At my place, we ran for the apartment door. Three steps inside, she wrestled me down, panting, tearing at my clothes. Ripped my shirt and trouser buttons getting them off. Then she was on top and grinding.

"Hit me," she said, out of nowhere. "Hit me hard."

On the rough carpet, in the darkness, I was falling. She rocked harder; sweat trailed down the cleft between her breasts. She hunched further, pulled my hand to her face.

"Hit me. *Please*."

And I did. Once, twice, then a third time—in the face. Left the imprint of my fingers on her dusky-colored cheek.

It gave her what she needed. She went rigid, then collapsed to the floor. Rolling to her side, she started crying.

I spent a long time in the bathroom, washing my hands. She knocked, kept knocking.

"Jeffrey, I have to talk to you," she said.

Eventually she went away.

I never called. All that remains is a pair of black silk stockings folded in a drawer. Sometimes, when the light is gray or the night more empty than usual, I take them out. Then, I trace their crooked seams.

Ian Randall Wilson is a faculty member at the UCLA Extension. His short stories and poetry have appeared in many journals, including the Gettysburg Review, Alaska Quarterly Review, and the North American Review. Ian was awarded the Cera Foundation Poetry Award in 1994, and first fiction collection, Hunger and Other Stories, was published by Hollyridge Press.

In Flight

Of course, they meet on a plane. The empty seat between them seems, at first, like a blessing—welcome elbowroom, a comfortable boundary. As she settles into 10C, they mumble *hello*.

After that you know what happens. They fall into—no, not love, stop being so romantic—they fall into silence, he with his BlackBerry, she with her book. She is thinking of her husband, at home with the baby, and feeling guilty. No matter that this trip is business, entirely legitimate. Leaving them, even for a few days, feels like a betrayal.

Before her daughter was born, she would have been thinking about the man in 10A, considering the possibilities: the casual conversation with its subtle undertones of desire; the lengthening glances; the eventual move to 10B, ostensibly to peer out the window, the light pressure of his arm against hers. It's a long flight, five hours. There would be time for everything to happen in an unhurried, natural fashion. It was all much easier before the baby, before there was so much at stake.

Glancing over, she notices that his legs look good in his jeans. His hair has personality. The wire-rimmed glasses have the probably-intended effect.

He, meanwhile, is thinking about a girl in Atlanta, the warm smell of her neck. Also, about football. Please, don't hold this against him! By football I mean the World Cup, which will be happening during his birthday, June 23. He's thinking about the barbecue he'll have in his garden in Oxford (England, not Mississippi). He'll make spiced pork balls with chipotle sauce, he'll serve a nice Thai beer, and with any luck England will pull it together. He looks up, sees the woman watching him. Caught, she smiles slightly. Is he imagining things, or is it a vaguely sexual smile, an acknowledgement? Perhaps she's not as uptight as he first thought. With American women, it's so hard to tell. She looks like she just rolled out of bed, which she probably did, because it's a god-awful early flight. Still, there's this: when she was placing her bag in the overhead bin, her T-shirt lifted to reveal the pale swirl of her navel. Above the low waistband of her jeans he glimpsed the rise of her pelvic bones, the lace edge of her underwear—dark blue. God, he thinks, this world of women! They're everywhere.

"Coming or going?" she asks.

"Going."

"To?"

"Atlanta. Yourself?"

"Boston," she says, before returning to her book. A pinprick of cold air blasts from the overhead fan.

He looks out the window, at the green hills and blue bay. There is a pleasant, unexpected awkwardness as they silently wait for the plane to begin taxiing.

At this moment—it is not so improbable!—their thoughts converge. They are both thinking that it is a fairly long flight, five hours. A great deal can happen in five hours. Really, there is no need to rush.

Michelle Richmond's books include the award-winning story collection The Girl in the Fall-Away Dress *and two novels,* Dream of the Blue Room *and* A Year of Fog. *Her fiction has appeared in Glimmer Train, Playboy, the Mississippi Review, and elsewhere. She lives in San Francisco, where she publishes the online literary journal Fiction Attic.*

ALL IT LOVES

It is dawn, but the sun is still lying on the floor at the top of the stairs. Last night, I thought I heard a woman in a long dress coming up to kiss me goodnight: Mother. But it was the sound of the sun's petal brushing against the stairs, fluttering over the handrail.

I had made the bed, white crispy sheets, a soft pillow, a feathery blanket. However, the sun could not make it to the room. It dropped on the floor, exhausted, an enormous yellow chrysanthemum picked, smelled and thrown.

Now it is dawn, and I am looking up. The room next to mine is closed and silent. Mother's translucent face shutting eyes between white sheets. Outside, the darkness retreats to its shelter, and a pale light, the leftover of yesterday's summer, drifts uncertain in the air. It enters through our cracked-open door and peers at the sun.

I tickle one yellow leaf and then another; I pull at the third but straighten it with regret. The sun opens an eye and takes in the hesitant light, the visitor. It enfolds the light with care and lets it breathe for another moment of dawn. I stand against the goose-bumped wall and watch the sun open up, letting go of the light it has nurtured, releasing all it loves.

Avital Gad-Cykman lives and writes in Brazil. Her work has been published in Glimmer Train, McSweeney's, Prism International, Other Voices, Happy, Stand Magazine, Stumbling, and in the anthology Stumbling and Raging: Politically Inspired Fiction (McAdam/Cage). Her work has also appeared online in Salon, Zoetrope All-Story Extra, Salt Hill Review, 3:AM, In-Posse Review, and elsewhere.

When there is no love,
nothing is possible.

HEADLESS ANGEL

Beth was three months pregnant when we went to France on our honeymoon. The trip represented our promise not to let the baby change who we were, not to forget that there was so much world, all around, waiting. Then in Normandy, strolling down to the beach for lunch, we saw a woman dive from a fourth-floor window and die on the sidewalk, right across the street. It was horrible, a shock out of nowhere on a gorgeous sunny day. People ran to the rag-doll body, yelling for a doctor, yelling for the police. But it was hopeless. Beth trembled against me in a way she never had before; I knew she was remembering her younger sister who had killed herself. Hugging each other hard, Beth and I walked to the shore. Young men in tiny bathing suits played volleyball on the sand, oblivious to what had happened two hundred feet away.

"It'll be all right," I said finally, to both of us. I put the untouched bread and cheese in my backpack, though I was very hungry. I squinted against the glare off the Atlantic. The water was cold here, all year round.

"Right," Beth said.

The next day we drove the abbey road, along the Seine. The river flowed slow and perfect in the morning mist. We stopped at the Abbaye de Jumièges and paid to enter the magnificent ruin, roofless walls and white stone spires reaching for the sky.

Beth disappeared.

I found her in a courtyard staring at a decapitated marble angel, its childlike hands palm-to-palm in prayer, the front of its bare feet broken off and worn as smooth as a windowsill polished by generations of elbows.

Beth touched the angel's wings. "Vacation's almost over, lover," she whispered. "Soon we have to fly home."

Our fingers intertwined on the cold, hard stone.

Tom Hazuka is a professor of English at Central Connecticut State University. He has published two novels, The Road to the Island and In the City of the Disappeared, and one book of nonfiction, A Method to March Madness: An Insider's Look at the Final Four (co-written with C.J. Jones). His young adult novel, Last Chance for First, will be published in 2008. He has co-edited three other short story anthologies: A Celestial Omnibus: Short Fiction on Faith (Beacon Press); Flash Fiction (W.W. Norton); and Best American Flash Fiction of the 21st Century (Shanghai Foreign Language Education Press). His short fiction, essays, and poems have appeared in many literary magazines.

La Guaca

There was a man who owned the finest restaurant in the village. Though no name adorned the establishment, the villagers dubbed it La Guaca, the tomb. The man, as well, had no name, at least none that the villagers knew. He was a complete mystery, a man apparently with no family, no origin, no history. They called him El Huérfano, the orphan.

One evening, as the villagers gorged themselves on enchiladas, tamales and other delectable dishes, El Huérfano rose from his usual seat at the corner table and cleared his throat. The room fell into silence.

"I plan to take a bride," said El Huérfano to the startled villagers. "But," he cautioned with a raised, elegant finger, "she must be perfect in every way."

Most of the families had at least one unmarried daughter because the Revolution had taken from this earth most of the village's eligible young men. So, this announcement raised great hope in the hearts of the parents and their daughters.

"I invite all of the village's Señoritas to feast here tomorrow night," said El Huérfano. "No one else may come. And I will choose my wife from among the guests."

"How will you choose?" an older woman asked. But El Huérfano turned and disappeared through a back door. A great cheer filled the void because this mysterious but wealthy man would make someone's perfect daughter a bride.

The next evening, all of the village's single women swarmed La Guaca dressed in all their finery. Though El Huérfano was not the handsomest of men, times were hard and there was little chance of living a comfortable life without a marriage of convenience. Remarkably, all of the women found seats in La Guaca and they waited. The tables sighed with great platters of food and bottles of fine brandy. Finally, after what seemed an eternity, El Huérfano appeared.

"As you know," he began, "I search for the perfect wife."

The room murmured in anticipation.

"Before you sits a great feast," he continued, noticing one particular beauty who sat motionless amidst the others. "But it is poisoned."

A horrified gasp rose from the young women.

"The poison is so potent, it will kill in a matter of minutes." El Huérfano now whispered, "But it will not harm a perfect woman. If you wish to leave, please do. Otherwise, enjoy your dinner."

Only one woman stood and left. The others slowly served themselves and commenced eating, each believing that she would survive. After a few minutes, the first victim fell. And then there was another and yet another. Finally, only the most beautiful woman was left. She stood and walked to him.

"You shall be my wife," he said as he moved his lips to hers.

She leaned forward and they kissed. El Huérfano could taste the wonderful feast from the beauty's lips. But then his eyes bulged and he fell back.

"No!" he sputtered as he dropped to the floor.

"Yes, my love," said the beautiful woman. "Yes."

Daniel A. Olivas is the author of Devil Talk: Stories (Bilingual Press, 2004), Assumption and Other Stories (Bilingual Press, 2003), The Courtship of María Rivera Peña: A Novella (Silver Lake Publishing, 2000), and a children's book, Benjamin and the Word/Benjamin y la palabra (Arte Público Press, 2005). His writing has appeared in several anthologies and many publications including the Los Angeles Times, El Paso Times, MacGuffin, Exquisite Corpse, Tu Ciudad, Vestal Review, and the Jewish Journal. He is currently editing Latinos in Lotus Land: An Anthology of Contemporary Southern California Literature, to be published by Bilingual Press in 2007. His website is http://www.danielolivas.com.

MEMENTO MORI

The baby was born with a hole in her spine, and all the love that Estelle and Art poured into it was not enough to seal her tiny soul inside. Estelle—daughter of Florida, tall, thin and elegant—chain-smoked cigarettes in a silver holder and clung to Art's broad chest. She swallowed her grief, buried it in her vacant womb, polished it to a fist-sized pearl with unshed tears. A year later, it thrust itself into the surgeon's hand, leaving her barren.

I was born then, Art's sister's first girl. Baby-simple, I warmed to my aunt's caresses, not knowing I had stolen them.

Estelle and Art lived exotic in the brick jungle of Chicago, while I tended cows and schoolbooks. I saw them little. But in my tenth summer, they drove me with them to Florida. My mother said, "You have always been her favorite."

I cared nothing for the Why. Wild with ocean, shoes leaking sand, I body-surfed breakers and gobbled crayfish, and gaped as Estelle's tiny mother dipped snuff from a jeweled snap-top box. I filled my Brownie camera with wonders: segregated beaches, motels. Tobacco fields. Lookout Mountain. Art and Estelle; her regal poise; his frayed black stogies. Leaning on the Buick. His broad hand brown on her lady-white shoulders. Her bobbed black hair against his muscled arm.

Summer died. I stumbled fiercely about the barn, kicking chickens, stabbing cows with truculent stares.

For Art, winter brought death. Mother told me one wind-whipped school afternoon: his heart.

I felt loss. But I was selfishly young, filled with books and plans and, yes, the dreaded cows. Estelle pulled Art's old Buick up to the snowbound house. Her head high, she drew me to her narrow smoky bosom, laid a scarlet-tipped finger on my cheek and searched my eyes—for what, I did not know. Then she nodded and drove away. To replant herself in Florida, with her mother.

I grew away, fast-forwarding from farm and family, grew like Jack's beanstalk through clouds into a blue sky of airplanes, into far-flung agoras and feluccas and minarets and yurts. I fell in love in a jungle, far from cows; we shimmered with life and purpose and made perfect children.

In Florida, a past land, Estelle's mother shrank and faded away. I sent the obligatory letter; I received pictures—Estelle tall, pole-thin, rail-straight, long cigarette held split-fingered at her chin, now minus the holder. Alone. Old. In her new Buick. Her letter spoke, strangely, of Art: Ah, I miss the man. He knew me.

She was eighty when her smoke-brittled bones crumbled. Estelle was gone, drifted ash, before I reached Florida. Side by side, my mother and I boxed away chic size-two dresses for charity in her haunted, orderly house.

In a bedroom redolent of pine and old smoke, buried deep beneath sweaters and lavender sachet, I found a small snow-white box.

Inside, cradled lovingly in rose-dotted tissue, lay hand-knit pink baby booties.

Susan O'Neill writes fiction and nonfiction, has been nominated twice for the Pushcart Prize, and has been named a notable author by Best American Essays. Her book, Don't Mean Nothing: Short Stories of Vietnam (Ballantine, 2001; Black Swan [UK], 2002; and UMass Press, 2004), was based on her year as an Army nurse during the Vietnam war. She lives in Massachusetts with her husband. Visit her online at http://www.susanoneill.us.

INFARCTION

I'm sitting on the nubby gold and brown brocade couch that
chafes my legs in the summer, watching Red Skelton with my
mother, cross-eyed Clem Kadiddlehopper capering pleadingly
before the camera, which is where I first learned that people
enjoy good-natured ignorance, look to it for reassurance that
they are wise, make reasoned and discerning judgments (something that has always made me feel sad and extraneous), and I
become suddenly and acutely aware of my heart beating, drum-
ming madly, a percussive warning that the enemy approaches
(I look at my chest to see if the insistent thumps are lifting my
shirt), and I begin to think that it is only this awareness, now
that the wire has been tripped, that will keep me alive, that
I now have the burden of being constantly mindful of every
beat lest, unremarked, this willful muscle ceases to contract
altogether, and I'll fall to the ground, limp as a dish towel,
victim of my own distractible nature, another lost child who
failed to recognize God when He came knocking at her body's
door. God is always muscling His way into my veins and joints,
and, like the good flagellant, I thank him for my pain, but this
is an ambush, boring into my preoccupied heart as I sit before
the snowy Motorola, and I am determined to be worthy of it.
I can tell as it hammers against my chest, a prisoner demand-
ing release, that my God-infested heart will use any excuse
to escape, any pretext to leap from my chest and beat a path
toward the door. It is a test. This causes me to inhale sharply,
and my mother turns to me, still grinning from watching Clem's
antics, and it's clear that she sees the stricken look creasing my
face, though I try to conceal my terror. But she is accustomed to
these looks by now—in fact, they became such a frequent occur-
rence that she took me to Dr. Yulich to see if this was normal, so

many unsettling sources of panic and dread in an eight-year-old girl—so she strokes my cheek and turns back toward the television, just as Dr. Yulich advised. Meanwhile my heart seems to have dislocated itself, pulled free of the tethers that keep it from sneaking off to somewhere else in my body, stowing away in one of its many hidden compartments, and I frantically finger my sternum, try to hold the crafty heart in place, and then I feel my lungs inflating with air, flaccid balloons that fill and empty with my shallow breathing, something *else* I must now monitor, and I gasp, paw at my throat, sit forward on the couch, plant my feet on the floor, straighten my back. I turn to see my mother smile woodenly at the television, through the commercial, hands clasped in her lap, trying not to notice the mad child, the one who aches to be pure, arteries clogged with God, drowning in the body beside her.

Kellie Wells was awarded the Flannery O'Connor Award and the Great Lakes Colleges Association New Writers' Award for her collection of short fiction, Compression Scars. She is also a recipient of the Rona Jaffe Foundation Writer's Award for Emerging Women Writers. Her work has appeared in various journals, including the Kenyon Review, the Gettysburg Review, and Prairie Schooner. Her novel, Skin, was published in 2006 by the University of Nebraska Press, in their Flyover Fiction Series, edited by Ron Hansen. She teaches in the writing program at Washington University in St. Louis, Missouri.

Buddha's Happy Family Jewels

Jackie says, "Chinese food is supposed to mix together on the plate." I know him as Dave but he says he is Jackie. We are sitting in a bad-good Chinese place that uses quality grease. The centerpiece is a ripped silk flower and a wooden Buddha. The lunch in front of me has become orangecashew beefpork despite my efforts to separate it.

"I don't like it mixed up," I say. "I wish these plates had compartments."

Jackie shrugs. "It doesn't matter. It runs together anyway." He picks up the Buddha and strokes it thoughtfully. "His stomach is so smooth. And his head. No hair anywhere."

"I bet he has hairy testicles."

"I don't know if he has any at all," says Jackie.

"I've never patted the Buddha below the belt, but I think he does."

He hands me the figure. "I always thought the big belly was supposed to imitate early Goddess carvings. The miracle of life. Being a man would have been hard for him. I bet he tucks."

I rub the Buddha's belly. He feels reassuringly masculine. "I'm still sick in the mornings. We should have met for dinner instead. Or after the baby is born."

Jackie frowns. "Are you worried I won't give child support? I will, after I pay for the surgery."

"I don't care about the money," I say, setting the Buddha down. "I'd rather have you come home."

Now Jackie picks up the Buddha and studies it carefully. "I'm sorry, but I can't. It's not you, I swear. It's all me."

"I still love you."

Jackie sighs. "You never knew me. And that was my fault." He takes ten bucks and a tube of lipstick out of his purse. He puts the money on the table and freshens his lipstick. He smacks his lips in my direction, in a kiss that's not meant for me. He stands up and glides out the door, his high heels clattering on the tiled floor.

Vylar Kaftan's work has appeared in Strange Horizons, Lenox Avenue, and Raven Electrick. She attended Clarion West in 2004, and currently volunteers as a mentor for young writers through the Absynthe Muse program. Visit her website at http://www.vylarkaftan.net.

SLEEP-OVER

Ed and I were making out by candlelight on the couch. Pammy was in my bedroom with Ed's brother; she wanted to be in the dark because her face was broke out.

"We were wishing your head could be on Pammy's body," Ed said. "You two together would make the perfect girl."

I took it as a compliment—unlike Pammy I was flat chested. Ed kissed my mouth, throat, collarbone; he pressed his pelvis into mine. The full moon over the driveway reminded me of a single headlamp or a giant eyeball. Ed's tongue was in my ear when Mom's car lights hit the picture window. Ed slid to the floor and whistled for his brother who crawled from the bedroom on hands and knees. They scurried out the screen door into the backyard and hopped the fence. Pammy and I fixed our clothes and hurriedly dealt a hand of Michigan rummy by candlelight.

"You girls are going to ruin your eyes," Mom said, switching on the table lamp. When Mom went to change her clothes, Pammy whispered that she'd let Ed's brother go into her pants. Her hair was messed up, so I smoothed it behind her ear.

"Too bad this isn't in color," Pammy said later, when we were watching *Frankenstein*. While the doctor was still cobbling together body parts, Pammy fell asleep with her small pretty feet on my lap. I stayed awake, though, and saw the men from the town band together and kill the monster.

7:23 P.M.

Paint your nails. Inhale. Exhale slowly. Let the paint dry.

It's easy. This waiting.

Once the nails are dry, do the dishes. Slowly, deliberately. Dry each plate, each cup, each bowl. Close each cabinet door without letting it make a noise. Inhale.

Vacuum straight lines in the carpet. Dust with the kind of precision your mother would be proud of. Exhale.

Think, think, think.

Check the machine for messages. When the solid red light is still solid and red, put your hands on your hips. Look up. Keep looking. Stand that way until your whole life clings to itself and settles at the base of your spine.

Take a shower. Exhale.

Look at yourself in the mirror. Suck in your stomach. Stick it out as far as it will go. Get dressed.

Imagine the phone will ring the minute you make yourself rush out the door.

Rush out the door.

As you walk to the bus stop, recreate the message word for word. It ends with love and a soft click.

Wait for your bus. Look up the street and down. See hope in the stoplight, the car alarm, the corner deli's lighted sign. Watch the bus come screaming in.

Let it leave the curb without you. Let it pull away.

Squint. Raise your hand to your eyes.

Wait for the next and the next and the next.

Sherrie Flick is author of the award-winning flash fiction chapbook I
Call This Flirting (Flume Press, 2004). Her work has been published in
numerous literary journals, including North American Review, Prairie
Schooner, Puerto del Sol, and Quick Fiction. Her anthologies include,
Sudden Fiction: The Mammoth Book of Minuscule Fiction (Mam-
moth Press, 2003), Flash Fiction Forward (W. W. Norton, 2006), and
New Sudden Fiction (W. W. Norton, 2006). She lives in Pittsburgh,
Pennsylvania, where she is co-founder and artistic director of the Gist
Street Reading Series, (http://www.giststreet.org).

Bruce Taylor

EXERCISE

Take a story from real life, one you are having trouble focusing.
Cut the story in half. Cut it in half again. What you're left with
is the essentials of the story you will be able to see more clearly.

(257 words)

They have said nothing to each other for weeks except what
matters to the day, the children, the budget or the dog. He is
upstairs at his office window. She is reading in a chaise longue
in the shade some book her recently widowed mother gave
her. She sighs, he imagines, at how it was an easy mistake for
a young girl to make, a less likely error, perhaps, for a man so
much older.

Who remembers mostly a white dress, a waist your hands
could fit around, the scent of Juicy Fruit and Noxzema. When
he asks what's wrong, she always says she's happy; the only
thing is, if he were sometimes a little happier a little more
often too…

What she thinks of him now he doesn't even know, but
fears it's so much less than what she thought at first, when he
was what he can't imagine now, and obviously isn't to her now,
and why and why? In the grief of his fifties, hard liquor sits
him down to pray.

They treat each other as tenderly at least as they'd treat a
relative or friend, a needy stranger or the obligatory guest.
Whatever it is they might be discussing escapes to the underside of the birch leaves in the gathering breeze. The lights
across the river are brighter and seem more distant than the
stars. The swallows give way to the bats and a tiny spider spins
at the ruined screen a web someone less desperate might be
tempted to take as a metaphor.

(128 words)

They have said nothing to each other for weeks except what matters to the day, the children, the budget or the dog. He is upstairs at his office window. She sighs, he imagines, at where love has led her and how it was an easy mistake for a young girl to make.

He remembers a white dress, a waist your hands could fit around, the scent of Juicy Fruit and Noxzema—he wants to ask her what she remembers.

They treat each other as tenderly at least as they'd treat a relative or friend, a needy stranger or the obligatory guest. Whatever it is they might be discussing escapes to the underside of the birch leaves. The lights across the river are brighter and seem more distant than the stars.

(63 words)

They have said nothing to each other for weeks except what matters to the day. She sighs at where love has led her. He remembers a white dress. They treat each other as they'd treat a stranger. Whatever they might be discussing escapes to the underside of the birch leaves. The lights across the river are brighter and more distant than the stars.

Bruce Taylor's poetry, fiction, and translations have appeared in such places as the Chicago Review, the Exquisite Corpse, Light, the Nation, Nerve, the New York Quarterly, Poetry, the Vestal Review, and E2ink-1: the Best of the Online Journals 2002. His current project is a short fiction series called Story Is, of which this selection is a part.

FAMILY THERAPY

Gathered together in her office, we are a mysterious centrifugal force dispersed around the bland interior. Earlier, each of us had a separate session of our own. Now, the therapist sits in our circle, trying for eye contact to reassure us that she is with us for the long haul.

To be here, my husband needed to inform his secretary to hold this time open, to arrange a continuance on the Haythorpe case, to leave work without a bulging briefcase that keeps him in our downstairs study past my bedtime, preparing briefs and citing precedent past midnight most nights, lights blazing.

To be here, our daughter had to deign to emerge from her bedroom whose canopied bed is hung with mosquito netting she refuses to discuss, emerge from behind dark glasses, from under headphones, arms crossed over a Marilyn Manson t-shirt, one of thirty on the floor.

To be here, our son was subjected to another fatherly, law-yerly outburst no longer effective, although my husband hasn't figured this out yet, so I threatened cancellation of the DSL line, and the withdrawal of help with college applications scattered around his bedroom where he sleeps beside his monitor, all lights on.

To be here, I needed to make the appointments, write my husband a reminder, watch my daughter write the time and place on the palm of her hand, and stick a post-it on my son's computer. I needed to leave my rosewood desk where I write my weekly column on new restaurants, to forego meditation, to leave my book on the guest room bed, where I frequently sleep or daydream of the ghost who wanders through the house, long skirts swishing against hard-edged Danish furniture, lantern held yearningly high in her search for something or someone. I needed to entice the family to assemble, cajole us to arrive today at the same time to hear just where we go from here.

But first, the therapist says, she has one other thing to say. Then she laughs, a tinkly laugh she surely would have stifled had she realized how dismissive she sounds about the only thing she could have said to send us out of her office forever, not cured—cured of what, anyway?—but a family again.

Giggling, my daughter rises to announce, "That settles that." Her brother follows her out the door asking, "Was it pearly white?" and then their father stands and looks around as if precedent has somehow failed him, but he'll give it another chance. He follows the kids, calling, "Let's all go to lunch." The therapist is clearly feeling left out, but what can I do but eventually pay her bill? As I gleefully join my family, I replay what the therapist said, moments ago, when we were still gathered in her circle, before we became a family again, hysterical with complicity and relief.

She said, "Before we begin, I want each of you to know: you have all seen the ghost."

Pamela Painter is the author of two short story collections, Getting to Know the Weather *and* The Long and Short of It. *She is also the co-author of the widely-used textbook* What If? Writing Exercises for Fiction Writers. *Her stories have appeared in numerous anthologies and journals such as the* Atlantic, Harper's, Kenyon Review, Mid-American Review, Ploughshares, Quick Fiction, *and* Night Train. *Painter serves on the advisory boards of Grub Street, RoseMetal Press, and Castle Hill, and is a founding editor of StoryQuarterly. She lives in Boston and teaches in the writing, literature, and publishing program at Emerson College.*

There is yet time enough for you
to take a different path.

A Room of Frozen Dust

I meet you in Scarborough. The station is packed with passengers waiting for the next train south. Day by day, the ice is creeping over the earth, unimpeded by the swollen sea. It has obliterated whole cities. Across the channel, it encroaches on the highest peaks. Soon it will join glaciers.

I've booked the last room in the hotel still open to visitors. In the hallway two maids are finishing their work. One ducks her head as we pass. The other stares. "She's rude," I whisper, putting my arm around your shoulders.

Your eyes walk straight through me, avoiding the part that hurts. My hands tremble and the key is difficult. Someone has stripped the room. The telephone has been disconnected. At least the sheets are clean. We cover the window with my leather coat. We do not talk about the advancing wall of ice.

There is a candle on the dresser. You light the long wick so the flame burns high. It's hottest at the top, you say, and hold my hand over it, laughing when I pull away.

You tell me how your dreams are mashed up inside. Fix me, say your fingers when they come to free my belt. Your hair is pale moonlight. I touch it with a whisper, "Nothing is irrevocable."

Your dusky roses died, all bitterroot and weed. When I touch your thigh, you close your eyes.

I wake to a room of frozen dust, a blurred note by the telephone. It is a long way back to the station. I walk past the docks, where all is a shifting curtain of mist. The boats are ghosts on an anthracite sea. Ice spiders come with the fog. They spin pale webs over the street lamps, lambent rainbows on frosted glass.

I wonder if you fear the cold. If you feel it.

Marge Ballif Simon is a freelance writer-poet-illustrator for genre and mainstream publications such as the Pedestal Magazine, Strange Horizons, Flashquake, Aeon, Flash Me Magazine, Dreams & Nightmares, From the Asylum, and Vestal Review. Her self-illustrated poetry collection, Artist of Antithesis, was nominated for a Bram Stoker Award in 2004. Marge is former president of the Science Fiction Poetry Association and now serves as editor of Star*Line. Her website is http://hometown.aol.com/margsimon.

Sonya Taaffe

Skins on Sule Skerry

When first they met, he stole her skin: cheaper than a wedding ring and twice as clear. All the soft storm greys, marbled silver and watered white silk, her throat, her thighs, the arch of her spine bundled away and collecting dust, became the secret kept at the crux of their hearts. There is a closet in the attic she does not touch. There are words they do not speak. Love is possession, the old word for this act committed between sheets with no smell of the sea on them; sometimes she tastes her tears and imagines the rising tide slipping against her mouth, his insistent rhythm the buffeting waves; he wants to know why she always keeps her eyes closed. So he has her, and has her somewhere in the house: her heart and her shadow, her soul and her self, the tidal core of her longing. When he is away at work, she wanders the house alone. A stranger looks back from the mirror's glass.

In the lonely afternoons, she writes laments for the grey salt gulf that was her home. She is not much of a poet. But he does not read them; fear averts his eyes. Lately the earth itself has begun to pull at her, soil crusting the soles of her feet, his seed a stone in her belly; she would sink, land-gravid, if ever the waves rose and spilled about her again. She pictures a blind fish, floating in the saline dark, and envies it. Tides come and go deep within her. The roar of the blood-sea sounds in its ears that cannot yet hear. Her child: his child: tightening the knot never tied at the altar, spurious claim on her substance. Her palms are bleeding from the clench of her fingernails. In the attic somewhere, no one sees the silver dip and shine of light on her fur.

Clumsily, he caresses her swelling flesh and says he loves her. Will it have her eyes, depth-dark? Her hair, the color of rain? He will love it because it is hers. He will never lose her. He knows how she feels. His language rattles like pebbles in her mouth, sparse, dry, skinned of meaning; she cannot answer him. Instead she spits in the dust at his feet. In the mornings, nausea like sea-sickness grips her. She rises unsteadily, one hand on the side of the sink, and feels the earth heave beneath her. Her sight pitches. The taste of her own tears no longer comforts her.

Daily she takes the bus down to the harbor; and in the breathing darkness at night, she dreams of drowning.

Note from the author: Seal-men seduce human women and their children are ill-fated heroes. Fishermen steal the skins of seal-women and bring them ashore as brides. These are the stories of the selkies, who shed their skins to become men and women on the land, who must have their sealskins to return to the sea. You will have to decide how this one ends.

Sonya Taaffe has a confirmed addiction to myth, folklore, and dead languages. Her poem "Matlacihuatl's Gift" shared first place for the 2003 Rhysling Award, and a respectable amount of her short fiction and poetry was recently collected in Postcards from the Province of Hyphens and Singing Innocence and Experience, both from Prime Books. She is currently pursuing a PhD in classics at Yale University. Updates, reminiscences, and memory can be found at http://sovay.livejournal.com.

Lamp

"Darling, I am completely in love with this lamp."

While she holds up the lamp I try to remember the last time she said she loved me. I know she's told me eight hundred and seventy-two times. In the beginning, she would say several "I love you's" in succession, so it was a challenge, but I never lost count. Time, though, sometimes confuses me. Was it three years ago, or five, since she loved me last?

She stares at me, Prada pump tapping, holding a lamp up for my approval. Actually, for permission. She has asked permission for twenty-eight other lamps, and I have given permission for all twenty-eight. She doesn't have a credit card or checkbook, though; it's all in my name, so she has to ask every time. She doesn't demand. She isn't a demander.

They call these Tiffany lamps, the ones with the stained glass and excessive prices. I know this because nineteen of the twenty-eight lamps already in the house are Tiffanies. This one she holds is blue and green. Beyond it, I stare at the blue curve of her breast, her sculpted green shoulder. When she lowers the lamp, sighing, her skin returns to normal and her white pants from Donna Karan turn green and blue.

I'm remembering what she used to look like, when I met her, so young and tiny, tanned teenaged wrists jangling with cheap silver bracelets stacked on, jeans tattered at the hems, pink tank top and enormous smile. I have seen her smile eighty-one thousand, seven hundred and thirty-four times. She has smiled at me forty-two thousand, one hundred and twelve of those times. Mostly I see her smiling at her friends, waiters, other guests at parties, valets, her manicurist, her hairdresser. The last time she smiled at me was last week, when I bought her a vase (number of vases currently in our home: forty-four. Number of vases on display and housing flowers: two).

I still have those jangling bracelets. She threw them in the trash and I found them. The bracelet on her wrist now cost four thousand dollars. She smiled at me then, too. I like it when she smiles.

"I'm not getting any younger," she says. I flinch. She's so beautiful. She holds the lamp up again, this time at face level, so that her cheek turns blue and her blonde hair turns green. I think about her appointment next week, where they will anesthetize her and slip two saline-filled bags into her chest. I can't think of the knife cutting into her skin. I want to steal her away, back to the day I met her, when she wore K-Mart flip-flops and smiled all the time, when she wore her pretty skin and hair and breasts so easily, like she was born with them.

Sarah Arellano has been published in Playboy, as well as in several online and print literary magazines. She lives with her family in Irvine, California.

BEACHED

She's taken the car he doesn't know where. She's gone off again. No, they don't have another car. No, he cannot say where and no, he does not think she will call, or write a note retrospectively…

Why does she have to do this? Why is it so difficult to write out on a scrap of paper, tape it to the door: I've gone to--------. I'll be back by-------. Surely one can be spontaneous, feel free, but also keep one's partner informed? No, not possible. Quite impossible for her.

He makes himself a cup of coffee. Strong as he likes it, no milk or sugar. For all he knows, she's gone off to get herself a cappuccino somewhere. As if coffee tastes better in a public place than home-brewed in their kitchen.

There was that time they'd stopped at a local favorite for lunch—they were on vacation, a small town in New Brunswick—a lovely screen porch, tables with vases of flowers, but no, she chose the indoor part of the restaurant. He'd relented. But felt the need to ask: Why, on a beautiful summer day—?

She shrugged. "There are more people here."

Exactly. Just the reason for getting away.

Like when they'd arrive at the beach together, he'd immediately head down to the end, where few people sat, where a slow rivulet of water tricked down the rocks. But he could feel her at his side, not quite with him—tugging invisibly—in the other direction.

"What?" he asked.

"I thought we might sit over there, where the other people are—"

Is it a fatal flaw? That she is drawn to people and places, while he is pulled toward the removed, remote, the private, and—it seems to him—infinitely more beautiful.

It occurs to him that this is exactly what draws him to her: her own remoteness. "Other people I know might be bothered," he remembers telling her, early on in their relationship, a hike they'd taken somewhere—"by the fact that you go for such long periods without saying anything. It might unnerve them. It doesn't bother me though. I feel comfortable with that about you."

Yet he also saw how she could be with others: a certain volubility welled up inside her, a cascade of words—ones he hadn't been treated to in a good long while.

He wants to get in the car to drive to find her. Then remembers that she has it. The car.

He stands at the door, thinking he hears the rumble of its engine, far off, getting closer—

But no, it's nothing. A lawn mower or tractor working its slow progress toward him.

Jessica Treat is the author of two story collections, Not a Chance (FC2, 2000) and A Robber in the House (Coffee House Press, 1993 & 2004), and is completing a third. Her stories and prose poems have appeared in numerous journals and anthologies. She is the recipient of a Connecticut Commission on the Arts Award and is an associate professor of English at Northwestern Connecticut Community College. More information about her can be found at: http://fc2.org/treat/treat.htm.

BEER AND GUNPLAY

The plan has always been this: Friday we drink the beer, Saturday we cook the chicken, and Sunday we shoot the guns. Except for an occasional holiday, abortion or act of God, Linda and I have been doing these things every weekend for almost three years.

The door slammed shut. It was Linda with the Budweiser and chickens. "How'd it go today?" I yelled over the stereo.

"Good," she yelled back. "I bought a case of Brown's Amber for tonight."

I didn't understand a word she was saying. I wanted to hear about Budweiser, or maybe Miller. "What the hell are you screaming about?" I said.

"Brown's Amber," she said, after she turned down the music. "It's a micro-brew. It's something different."

Linda has the longest, reddest hair you can imagine. And her favorite things to wear are tight jeans and tight t-shirts. When she gets close to me I can hardly think. I can barely see the world around us. I never know what I'm going to say.

"Screw the Brown's Amber," I said. "For your sake, it better be twice as good as Bud. And it better go with chicken."

"I got salmon," she said. "And we can drink all the Brown's tonight because I bought wine for the fish." Then she sat on my lap.

I was pissed, but I still wanted to kiss her. I wanted her to remember what we were. I wanted to make her forget about Brown's Amber and New Age fish. But I couldn't. Somehow I had gotten a mouth full of Linda's hair.

She rolled off my lap and onto the sofa. She took her hair with her and my throat was clear.

"I cleaned the rifle and the 40 caliber," I told her. "Everything's ready for Sunday."

"Sunday?" she said. "Oh yeah, Sunday." By then she had her shirt off and her jeans around her ankles.

Neno Perrotta is the author of a collection of short stories and poems titled Not One Thing About Science, published by Shenango River Books and edited by poet Jeanne Mahon. He has a BA in English literature and is passionate about reading, cult movies, and gardening. Neno is a member of the Fallen City writer's workshop, and welcomes e-mail at nperrotta1@netzero.net.

Pedro Ponce

THE ILLUSTRATED WOMAN

This was during better times. She called with her itinerary, reciting airline and gate numbers, her voice edged with hunger. I vacuumed, scrubbed, and laundered, shopped for two at the grocery store.

I waited at the gate, bouquet in hand. Next to me, a man was listening to the radio. The volume on his headphones was so loud I could hear Liz Phair comparing a lover to the explosion of a dying star.

She surprised me from behind and pressed her lips to my ear. We collected her bags and left the terminal. I splurged for a cab. While the driver cursed between lane changes, I could feel the rush of the chassis through her clenched thighs.

We were barely through the door when she led me to the bedroom. We fell together, a tangle of hair and tongues. The front of her jeans gave way to my fingers. She lifted her hips and slid them down. An unfamiliar mark appeared just above her hip bone.

What is that? I asked.

She smiled and gathered the hem of her sweater up with both hands. It's Chinese, she said. Do you like it?

I leaned closer. It was a symbol I recognized from bumper stickers and New Age bookstores. Two tailless fish—one black, one white—curled next to each other to form a circle.

I thought you hated needles.

I hate getting shots, she said. I've always wanted a tattoo.

She was drawn to its simplicity, centuries of wisdom inscribed on her skin. Two sides in opposition yet necessary to make a whole, discrete yet inseparable.

It made me think of you, she said. Besides, I didn't like any of the other designs. Can you imagine me with a sunflower on my ass?

What about my name? I said.

She wrestled me to the mattress, laughing. Silly, she said.

Later, I couldn't sleep. I got out of bed and sat by the window, watching her. Her legs kicked free of the sheets. With every breath, the shapes inked on her skin rose and fell, two halves and the indelible border between.

Pedro Ponce teaches at St. Lawrence University in Canton, New York. His short fiction has been published previously in Ploughshares, The Beacon Best of 2001, Vestal Review, DIAGRAM, and other publications.

Nebraska Men

In Nebraska men keep small colorful seashells in their mouths. When they speak, which isn't often, the soft roar of the ocean hums behind each word. In this way they are able to understand each distant coast. They are able to look across their long flat fields and imagine ships rocking slowly to port, see each grain ripening earnestly in the Midwestern sun, see time moving slowly in a line toward a very specific day.

The men stop and take their hats from their heads. They squint and whistle quiet tunes to songs they never knew. They smile. At night they ease their warm bodies into crisp white beds; they slowly rub their wives' backs. The men make soft circles with their rough hands and are gentle as winter wheat. Just as the women are about to sleep, they say goodnight to them; they kiss them gently.

When they wake, the men smile and say good morning to no one in particular, to their sleeping wives' tousled hair, to the mist clearing. They are quiet as they get out of bed, walk down their stairs. Nebraska men understand three a.m. and cows. It is their job.

When they get thirsty, they shift the shells to a soft hollow pocket that has formed in their cheeks. This gesture makes the smallest noise, barely audible over the whimper of a dog, the leaves on a cottonwood. The men turn on the faucet that is beside their sturdy graying barn. The water streams out in a high screech; they tilt their heads, stretch their thick red tongues.

It is then that the men come face to face with every single day in the year. They think how the one they're living today is no better than the last, how the next could possibly be the best one of all.

Sherrie Flick is author of the award-winning flash fiction chapbook I Call This Flirting (Flume Press, 2004). Her work has been published in numerous literary journals, including North American Review, Prairie Schooner, Puerto del Sol, and Quick Fiction. Her anthologies include, Sudden Fiction: The Mammoth Book of Minuscule Fiction (Mammoth Press, 2003), Flash Fiction Forward (W. W. Norton, 2006), and New Sudden Fiction (W. W. Norton, 2006). She lives in Pittsburgh, Pennsylvania where she is co-founder and artistic director of the Gist Street Reading Series (http://www.giststreet.org).

THE DIARY OF A SALARYMAN

Today I was promoted to a junior coordinator of coordinating activities. This means I'll get a 3% salary raise spread over five years. This also means I get to stay at work longer.

Wife bore quintuplets. Was allowed to take three days off from work. Brought home the laptop and had a telecon during the delivery.

My cubicle mate was laid off. Had to pick up his workload. When I bent over the crib today, one of the quintuplets peed in my face, from a foot away. I think it was a boy.

Wife e-mailed me a picture of the kids on their first day in school.

Was promoted to an associate coordinator of coordinating activities. This means I'll get a 4% salary raise spread over five years. This also means I get to stay at work longer.

Today I saw a car with five teenagers leaving my garage. They waved at me. Is wife renting the garage out?

The new cubicle mate had a heart attack. While they were getting him on the stretcher, had a conversation with a guy from across the aisle. His name was Pete, and he's been with the company for twenty-four years. Twenty years in the same cubicle. Same as me.

Was promoted to a senior coordinator of coordinating activities. This means I'll get a 5% salary raise spread over five years. This also means I get to stay at work longer.

They laid me off today. Counted the remaining Valiums. Only three. Not enough for suicide.

Took my five grandchildren to a ball game today. Had ice cream in the park. My chest was heaving and a strange sound came from my throat. I guess they call it laughter.

Wife retired. Ran out of Viagra, but had sex with her anyway. She screamed and raked my back with her nails. Wow. The last time she'd done that was nine months before the quintuplets were born.

Got a call from work today. They want to re-hire me. E-mailed them a pic of myself flipping the bird.

Today is my last diary entry for a while. Too busy planting strawberries in my garden. Wife takes a bubble bath. Means it's going to be a busy night, too.

Mark Budman has always been interested in short-shorts. To him, a short-short is not only a stepping stone to writing longer fiction, but a drawing power that could bring the busy masses back to literature. With his co-editor Sue O'Neill, he started Vestal Review, a magazine of flash fiction, back in March of 2000. Together with Sue, he has published thirty quarterly issues so far. Mark has been lecturing widely on the subject of flash. He taught it at Binghamton University, Ithaca College, Broome Community College, Art School Online, and is scheduled to be a panelist for the Saltonstall Foundation. Mark was born and raised in the former Soviet Union, but now resides in New York state. His novel My Life at First Try was scheduled for publication in May of 2008 by Counterpoint.

SNAPDRAGONS

What happened next was…well, no…The night before, I was out on the front porch with a beer trying to look at the sky, one of those nights when the stars…the moon and Venus together looked like the Turkish flag. There was a garden tool of some kind, a trowel, I remember thinking, on the steps, and it reminded me that I'd told her I would water the snapdragons. But the mint, the damn mint was growing everywhere, and the snapdragons had been dead for weeks.

I traded in the Buick for that truck, and four thousand bucks, all for a hundred thousand more miles and a ride like a hay wagon. But this is America, right, and if you can't throw away money on a truck…I loved that truck. It was blue except where it was rusty, and it pulled hard to the left when you hit the brakes, and the four-wheel drive ground like a nightmare, but I loved it. On the fire roads with her, ponderosa pines and sun-warmed granite. I thought it would be good luck.

The doctor appointment was at three o'clock. We got up early, and I looked up where the sliver of moon had crooked toward Venus. There were high cirrus clouds.

No, wait, the snapdragons weren't dead yet. That was when she asked me to water them. That morning. I was thinking, Which flag was it, the one with the moon and the star, or was it really Venus on the flag?

Water the snapdragons, okay? she said from inside. I was having coffee, and there were high cirrus clouds.

Yeah, I said, and stood there instead, listening to her move around in the living room. She picked up this and that. Nervous. We'd been trying for a long time. I was optimistic about this doctor. We were optimistic.

No, I couldn't have remembered telling her I'd water the snapdragons. That was the night before. Later I went and looked up what the thing was, the garden tool on the steps. It wasn't a trowel. I had meant to ask her, but I forgot. So no, I hadn't told her I'd water the snapdragons. That was after I first saw the thing on the steps. But it was still there when she said, Water the snapdragons, okay? I think that's why I forgot to ask her what it was.

It was my idea to take the truck. Good luck, I thought. The grinding was in the clutch, not the four-wheel drive, and if I'd paid attention when my dad told me about cars I'd have known. Anyway it kicked out of gear on Alameda and I jumped a little. We'd been trying for a long time. I was optimistic about this doctor. I was nervous, and I hit the brakes a little hard. We couldn't have crossed the center line that much.

The snapdragons hung on for a long time. Longer than I would have thought.

Alex Irvine has written five novels, including The Narrows and A Scattering of Jades. His short fiction is collected in Unintended Consequences and Pictures from an Expedition. He is an assistant professor of English at the University of Maine, and divides his time between Orono, Maine and New York City.

THE HOUSE AND THE HOMEOWNER

The homeowner found to his surprise that the home would not be owned.

"But I *paid* for you," he argued. He produced papers. "I *worked*," he said. "I went to work, every day, and I hated my job. See?" he said, as the house perused the papers.

"Mortgage. Investment. Equity."

The house just laughed. "What are these sheets of paper to my four-by-eight posts, to my beams and joists and two-by-four studs? What's your investment to my concrete foundation, your so-called equity to my earthquake retrofit?"

"Right, right, but I *paid* for that retrofit," the homeowner protested. "Don't you understand? My children grew up in this house. This is the house they grew up in, see?

"Roots," the house had to admit. But there was a twinkle in its upstairs windows.

"Exactly," the homeowner said, thinking he was getting somewhere. "Roots. The children."

The house coughed, clearing its closets. "But what," it asked, "are your children to my tree?"

"Tree?"

"The big one out front. Its roots have crawled around and under me. Now it towers over both of us. It doesn't wave papers in my face, just shades me through the summer, and cries on my shoulder every fall. *You* own me? You *own* me? I fucking *contain* you, Sir Homeowner."

The homeowner slammed the door behind him and sat in his car in the driveway, fuming. He didn't go anywhere, just sat in the driver's seat, behind the wheel, just sitting there, looking at his house and at the tree. The tree had a thick, straight trunk and long, sturdy limbs. He'd made tree houses in trees like that when he was a kid. He'd loved to sit in them with a cold drink and a good book on a hot summer day.

He closed his eyes.

He smelled leather, cigarette smoke, and dried coffee spills, with milk. "I own you," he said to his car.

L. E. (Dan) Leone writes a weekly humorous column about food and life for the San Francisco Bay Guardian. L. E. has published two books, The Meaning of Lunch (Mammoth Press, 2000), and Eat This, San Francisco (Sasquatch Books, 2002), as well as numerous stories in literary magazines and anthologies.

RAPTURE

The babysitter said the Rapture was coming, and it was coming now. "Sorry you'll be left behind, Jew boy," the babysitter said, even though his charge—namely me—was a girl. He unfolded himself from the couch where we had been watching *Let's Make a Deal*. A man in a lobster suit had just won a donkey, a real donkey hitched to a cart and wearing a sombrero. I wondered if the lobster man actually had to bring the donkey home. I wondered if the game show people taught him how to take care of it.

"Gotta go!" he said. "Gotta go to God!" He saluted me, clicked the heels of his white tennis shoes, and ran out the door.

I watched him race past the bay window, his arms waving over his head, his face upturned, laughing, like he was running to catch a bus, a bus that was going to take him to the best summer camp ever.

I called my mom at the insurance office where she worked. "What's the Rapture?" I asked. The only place I knew the word from was a Blondie song; it was on the radio a lot those days. The way Blondie sang the word scared me—kind of slow and drawn out, like she was falling asleep. And then there was a weird part I didn't really understand about an alien eating cars. I hoped an alien wasn't going to come eat our Cutlass Ciera now that the Rapture was here.

"Is that Daniel reading the Bible to you again?" she asked.

"No," I said, even though he had read a freaky passage to me earlier that day about a lady riding a serpent.

"It's a Christian thing," she said. "At the end of the world, Jesus is going to come take all the Christians away or something like that."

"What happens to the rest of us?" I asked.

"We all die a fiery death, I guess. I have to go, Janie. Be good." She hung up. She hung up on me even though we were both about to die. The phone squawked and squawked. It sounded like when the Emergency Broadcast System blats on the radio for a tornado or a flood. When I set the phone in its cradle, the quiet was almost more alarming. I looked out the window. The street was completely empty. The leaves on the trees were completely still. All the Christians were probably gone already. The fireball was probably on its way.

On *Let's Make a Deal*, a woman in an angel costume chose what was behind door number three. It was a boat, a glittery blue powerboat. She climbed up into the powerboat and I could see the jeans under her white angel robes. I could see her white tennis shoes, too, just like Daniel's. Christian tennis shoes. And she waved to the camera and I knew she was waving at me, and I knew she was waving goodbye.

Gayle Brandeis is the author of Fruitflesh: Seeds of Inspiration for Women Who Write, Dictionary Poems, and The Book of Dead Bird, which won the Bellwether Prize for Fiction in Support of a Literature of Social Change. Her second novel, Self Storage, will be published in 2007. She lives in Riverside, California with her husband and two children. You can visit her online at http://www.gaylebrandeis.com.

A man who desires to waste an hour of time hasn't discovered the value of life.

THE HUMAN PYRAMID

These neighbors of mine are driving me nuts. At first it was only a matter of clothing, then it got out of hand.

The big woman, the one with short hair, walks around naked talking on a cordless phone. There's always at least four or five little kids hanging on her legs or tagging along. The ones over three, they're naked, too. Babies wear diapers, thank God.

And four ponies and a llama they keep inside an electric fence. That's where you can always find the other woman, the one that most of the time wears at least underwear. She trains the ponies. I can't even guess what she does with the llama.

I asked the mailman, "What's with those people over there? What's their story?"

"Circus, I'm guessing," he said. "But they both get unemployment checks and letters to the kids from all over the world."

"Yeah. Sure," I said. "A world-renowned, nude circus." And to be honest, I was thinking Lesbians, too. But, since there were so many kids, I kept my mouth shut.

Now don't get me wrong. I've got nothing against nakedness. And I like kids and ponies as much as the next guy. It wasn't until a few weeks ago that the carnival-like goings-on became too much for me. That's when they started with the human pyramids. To be specific, the naked-human pyramids.

Every time they try, the whole thing comes crashing down. With those diapers on top it's a snow-capped mountain of naked flesh. It's a miracle no one ever gets hurt.

So, now I have to worry that they're not too bright. Hell, everyone knows you need at least one strong man to anchor a human pyramid. Maybe more.

That's what's driving me crazy. I even went over and asked them if they needed help. "I don't know about the nude business,"

I said. "But I could wear a bathing suit."

"Thanks," said the naked woman. "But, no thanks."

"How about a cape?" I said. "Tight shorts and a cape?"

"It's a family thing," said the "bra and panties" woman. "We're all in one, big happy family."

"Okay," I said. "But kids can get hurt. Somebody can get hurt."

"No we won't," yelled all the kids. "We never get hurt." They talked at the same time, like they'd been practicing since the day they were born.

When I turned to go home the kids laughed and ran to ride the ponies. I stopped and watched while some of them fell off and seemed to crack their heads on rocks. One of the babies tumbled onto the electric fence, laughing and delighted by the steam that danced up from her soggy diaper.

Neno Perrotta is the author of a collection of short stories and poems titled Not One Thing About Science, *published by Shenango River Books and edited by poet Jeanne Mahon. He has a BA in English literature and is passionate about reading, cult movies, and gardening. Neno is a member of the Fallen City writer's workshop, and welcomes e-mail at nperrotta1@netzero.net.*

THE HOUSE BROODS OVER US

i.

It was always the house with its crumbling eaves and weathered gables, its turrets and cupolas, its ornate fretwork and blank window eyes. It was the house with its sagging porticos and scattered trellises, the dark green vines trailing up the walls until their leaves turned sere and pale in the sun's heat.

It was always the house with its trenched history and ineradicable stains on the hardwood floors, vivid as birthmarks or faded as old scars.

ii.

I gathered the tools of the draftsman's trade with a serious intent, to learn the craft of the cartographer, to create a detailed map with a detailed legend, extensive and accurate, that would not only chart the limits of the house but give specific definition to its varied elaborations.

I set out to explore its multiple levels and seductive recesses, the shadow and substance of its rectilinear maze.

And you came with me in your wayward fashion, less than innocent and far from knowing, to share my explorations and test the dimensions of the world waiting beyond each wall.

iii.

We discovered hallways that led to nothing and others that turned back upon themselves. We entered rooms that were ordered and others in rank disarray.

You sat at a slender desk in a high drawing room that bathed your flesh in films of light. I paced beyond the carpet, dictating imaginary letters to composers and poets and heads of state.

We slept in a Victorian boudoir rich in its mock oriental

decadence, the portraits of dead sinners gracing our walls.

When I cut my hand on a splintered balustrade, your lips closed on the single drop of blood that welled in the lines of my palm.

iv.
When you turned back, gathering up the ball of yarn you had cleverly unwound to mark our distracted passage, I ventured farther to uncover corridors and cul-de-sacs that recalled ones we had visited together, standing rooms and sitting rooms and those stripped bare of all décor.

Was it days or only hours that I wandered before you found me crouched against a wall, unable to speak beyond a thirst that filled my body to its pores?

v.
We have settled in the rooms we inhabit and we do not stray past their boundaries. We stay close by our hearth and our fire beneath a mantel lined with framed images of these same rooms.

Beyond us we can feel the house brooding through days of neglect, the accumulated dust sifting into its bones, the sun shadows and moon shadows crawling across deserted floors, the shame in its solitude as it waits for a step to cut the silence.

Bruce Boston has received the Bram Stoker Award, a Pushcart Prize, the Asimov's Readers' Award, and the Grand Master Award of the Science Fiction Poetry Association. He is the author of forty books and chapbooks, including the novel Stained Glass Rain and the best-of fiction collection Masque of Dreams. Bruce lives in Ocala, Florida with his wife, writer-artist Marge Simon. For more information, please visit his website: http://hometown.aol.com/bruboston.

Michael A. Arnzen

THE CURSE OF FAT FACE

The kids called her fat face. And when she looked in the mirror, she saw they were right: her cheeks were as thick as thighs, her eyes pushed in plump like buttons pinching back the fabric of her overstuffed head.

She decided her face needed to diet. So she stopped feeding it attention.

She wore a scarf like a burka and hid behind sunglasses.

She avoided eye contact. Especially with mirrors.

She blinked. Often. She thought of this as a form of exercise, a way to melt away the cheek fat.

But mostly she just ground her teeth and did jaw exercises, which required many private conversations with herself at night, alone in a dark bedroom.

All this was much to the consternation of her mother, who listened intently at the door, trying unsuccessfully to make out the language.

Miraculously, the fat-faced girl reached her goal in just three weeks. The kids began leaving her alone, targeting other people's faces. Perhaps this was because she had become sallow and pale and scary.

Soon she found herself facially anorexic. Her button eyes now sank inside her cheeks like peach pits in empty pie pans. Her complexion waned; the black rings around her eyes triplicated concentrically. And her face fat was still there after all; she discovered it had simply moved to other parts of her skull, as if the cellulite had displaced to places where she'd pay more attention to it. It now hung in hammocks of flab from her jaw line and neck, like the dangly skin beneath an octogenarian's biceps.

At least, that's how the poor girl saw it. In her mother's eyes, she was simply thin.

A week later, her mother could take no more of her daughter's privacy and selfishness. She confronted her as she was gorging on *Cosmo* in the bathroom. The daughter confessed to spending sleepless nights with *Vogue*. She was bingeing on images of models between purges of attention, puking up pretty in ugly wet chunks. She knew she needed help and cried out to her mother.

But when they finally approached the hospital, racing in her mother's Cadillac, it was too late: mother went over a speed bump and her daughter's fat face fell right off the bone, sloughing down from her earlobes and chin and slurping into her lap before spilling on the floor of her mother's fine luxury car.

Before they covered her with a sheet, Mother thought she looked impeccable, like perfect teeth polished to the color of clean whitewall tires. When she returned home, she scooped her daughter's remaining skin off the floor mats and poured it into a shiny jar to place on her mantel. Everyone who visited was mesmerized by their reflection within its grotesque beauty.

Fat Face returned their gazes, feeding, pressing up against the glass a little more tightly with every passing day.

Michael A. Arnzen has won multiple Bram Stoker Awards for his horror fiction and poetry. He has been called "the master of minimalist horror" in the book Horror Fiction: An Introduction. Michael's collection of one hundred flash fiction stories, 100 Jolts: Shockingly Short Stories (Raw Dog Screaming Press, 2005), was published to much critical acclaim. He teaches Writing Popular Fiction at Seton Hill University near Pittsburgh, Pennsylvania. Visit him online at http://www. gorelets.com.

Lincoln Michel

THE MOUTH

The mouth on the top of Franz's head has a diameter of six inches. His address is 606 Hinton Avenue. The electricity tower next to his house is sixty feet tall. Franz is an accountant; he immerses himself in numbers and yet he has, so far, failed to figure out the significance of these repetitions.

The mouth can speak, but only German. The mouth is rude and gets Franz into trouble. After a grueling day of accounting, Franz steps into the elevator holding his briefcase neatly in front of his crotch. In the elevator is a shapely young woman in a blue power suit.

"*Du hast einen leistungsfähig Arsch,*" says the mouth.

The red handprint stays there for twenty minutes.

Franz wears a black bowler hat on the top of his head, to cover the anomaly. It was his grandfather's. Franz sits on a park bench musing over his fate. It is mid-May and Franz is the only person wearing a bowler hat. Franz is an accountant, but if he were an artist perhaps he would be more optimistic about his fate, given the history of famous faces obscured by apples and white birds. Perhaps he would view himself as walking art, perhaps.

A small squirrel, not cautious due to years of hand-feeding in the park, crawls along Franz's shoulder and wanders under his hat. It does not re-emerge. Franz weeps silently.

Franz sits nervously crinkling the thin white paper of the doctor's table. The doctor prods with his tongue depressor.

"It's a tumor," he says definitively.

"A…a tumor?"

"Yes, probably benign."

"Benign?! It just ate a squirrel."

"I meant it's not cancerous."

"Oh."

The mouth is learning some manners. Eating some particularly peppery salami, Franz sneezes.

"*Gesundheit,*" says the mouth.

Still, to Franz, the situation is becoming unbearable. He lies in bed at night asking God, "why?" But God does not answer him. If only there were someone for him, some kindred soul. Some woman with an eight-inch ear fixed to her dainty head who would hold him in her arms and listen, listen.

Lincoln Michel is a young writer from the southern United States. His flash fiction has appeared in journals such as the Mississippi Review, Quick Fiction, Pindeldyboz, and Vestal Review. He keeps an infrequently updated blog at http://lincolnmm.blogspot.com.

Aimee Bender

WRONG

When I saw the row of elephants crossing the road into the mouth of the very fat child, I knew I couldn't sit back anymore. I ran over and shook the child by its voluminous shoulders. Do you really think you're going to be happy being this huge? I yelled. I don't think so! Do you really think these elephants are going to sit quietly in your belly? I don't think so!

A gray trunk clung to the lip of the child's mouth, and then was sucked up and away into its cavernous throat. The child looked over at me, his eyes enormous circles, and swallowed. His face so happy, his belly trumpeting. It is miraculous, he said, and then his cheeks were drenched in tears.

Aimee Bender is the author of The Girl in the Flammable Skirt (Anchor Books/Doubleday, 1999), An Invisible Sign of My Own (Anchor Books/Doubleday, 2001), Willful Creatures (Doubleday, 2005), and she contributed to The Secret Society of Demolition Writers (Random House, 2005). Her stories have appeared in Granta, GQ, Story, Harper's, the Antioch Review, Vestal Review, and several other publications. She lives in Los Angeles, and her website is http:// www.flammableskirt.com.

CENTERFOLD

When her husband goes out for the evening, he leaves her, now seven months pregnant, at loose ends. She decides to clean out drawers. In the bottom drawer of his bureau she finds a several-months-old men's magazine. She opens to the "Dream Girl Centerfold" and uncovers a nude image of herself lying seductively on a beach.

Her legs stretched out in a V on the shore, her elbows prop her up from the beach so that her pelvis tilts out and her breasts arch back a little unnaturally. She smiles fetchingly over her shoulder. Behind her a fat blue wave curls itself into a glassy tube about to shatter on the sand.

On the next double page this image repeats exactly, except for a red line showing between her legs. On the next two pages the line becomes a stain in the sand. On succeeding double pages the stain spreads. She appears to be bleeding to death.

The provocative pose and her smile never change as she turns the pages, but the stain, a large dark spot, grows, reaching past her feet. On each double-page spread, the wind blows, lifting the ends of her hair.

Eventually, elbows still propping her up, her head lolls at a grotesque angle, her body rots, her skin turns to rags, as the wind continues to blow through her hair.

When the last of her flesh has disappeared, presumably picked off by gulls and ants, she is left as a skeleton propping herself up on the beach as the waves arch over. The stain has vanished. Her bones gleam sleekly in the sunlight. The figure of her skeleton cuts a stylish composition against ocean and sky.

She doesn't exist on the magazine's last two pages. The beach looks pleasant and inviting—the waves a cool, clean blue.

John Briggs is the author of Trickster Tales, a collection of stories published by Fine Tooth Press (2004). He has had over twenty-five stories published in chapbooks and literary magazines, and is the author and co-author of several nonfiction books on aesthetics and physics, including Fractals: The Patterns of Chaos (Simon & Schuster, 1992); Fire in the Crucible (St. Martin's Press); Seven Life Lessons of Chaos (HarperCollins), and Turbulent Mirror (HarperCollins, 1989), as well as Metaphor and the Logic of Poetry (Pace University Press, 1988). John is the senior editor of Connecticut Review, a distinguished CSU professor at Western Connecticut State University in Danbury, and co-founder of its MFA program in professional writing.

Divadlo

In Prague, in winter, the sky hangs low and smells of coal. Older people walk downtown with kerchiefs across their mouths like bandits. Younger people make out heavily on subway escalators, hands under skirts as they descend.

I am invisible. It is great and harrowing to be invisible.

The streets are made of cobblestones. Car tires sound like rain on a tent. Some days I don't speak to anyone, just walk around, taking pictures of things. Ride the subway out to Andel, where the walls are covered with Soviet-era murals. Big men with scythes and women in wheat fields. Skulk across Kampa Island, tell the snapping black-billed swans I'll be back after I learn the Czech word for bread.

It's *chleb*. Don't tell the swans.

There is a girl, but she has gone home to Gulfport, to its sticky heat and rising rivers. We won't meet again, because I am invisible. I have a heavy coat, and it has a hood.

Stare Mesto is the old town, full of old people. They are invisible, too. Invisible people can see each other. At the theatre, I get off the tram and spot one. A babushka. She has got her back to me. She is peering around the corner of a building, looking down the sidewalk for some unseen hand. I have learned the Czech word for theatre: it is *divadlo*.

This is a picture I will send to my girl back in Gulfport, the picture of the old woman peeking around a corner. It will make her smile, maybe.

I walk down the street, passing the old woman. She is clucking softly to herself. At the corner, I duck behind and affix the telephoto lens to my camera. In it, the street condenses. Things move fast, washing across the lens. I find the old woman in the viewfinder. Half her face around the corner, eyes cloudy with dementia. Searching the careless street for ghosts. Then she looks right at me, and smiles, and sees one.

Dave Fromm is an attorney in California and the author of Away Games, a memoir about playing basketball in the Czech Republic. He writes fiction in his spare time.

Chauna Craig

On Holiday

"Stay away from your future," I warned one last time, but Agata only laughed and pushed open the glass door to Madame Elaine's. Her scarf wagged like the pink-striped tail of an invented animal, and she disappeared into a room I imagined full of candles and incense and curious cold.

We were on holiday, delicious days where our life together was reborn each morning. Our choice in restaurants was unsullied by memories of surly waiters or wilted greens. Our strolls took us to streets with unfamiliar names. We could always get lost, and we agreed we wanted it that way. We were mayflies. Living, dying, hatching again, our minds lighting softly on every sensation—the song of the street vendor's cry, the smell of roast lamb, the brilliant neon nights—then flitting on. On holiday there were no children, no resentful mother-in-law watching them and wishing divorce would triumph over reconciliation, no failed affair with a sad woman who tasted of almonds and will never open her door again.

On holiday there can be no regrets because there is no past, and there should not be a future.

I tried to explain that to Agata when her eyes glowed with the promises on Madame Elaine's hand-painted sign: *Psychic Readings! Your Future... Today!* But she checked the bills in her wallet and said with an even smile I couldn't quite trust, "This has nothing to do with you."

"It's a waste," I called. "A risk."

I waited on a sidewalk scuffed by the soles of a million shoes and marveled over everyone who'd taken this same path. Chewed purple bubble gum hugged the concrete, but I didn't pry it up. I waited. And when my wife returned, she started to walk, with purpose. Her heels skirted the gum.

"What did she say?" I hurried to catch up.

"It's a secret." She called over her shoulder and her voice sounded years away. I walked even faster and my calves burned.

"Where are we going?"

She stopped. She studied the street signs. She studied me as if trying to look into my mind. Finally she pointed east where the brownstones huddled in the shadows of early evening. We'd eaten Mexican on that block. We'd liked nothing but the margaritas and the appetizing chips.

"But we've already been there," I complained, seeking another way.

Agata shrugged and walked on, confident of her direction, expecting I would follow or get lost on my own.

Chauna Craig is a professor of creative writing at Indiana University of Pennsylvania. Her stories have appeared in numerous literary magazines and anthologies, including Sudden Stories: A Mammoth Anthology of Miniscule Fiction. Her work has also been cited in Best American Essays and the Pushcart Prize anthology.

The day will come when you
have to search no longer.

Kay Sexton

Gatwick Blues

"So…" he folded his coat over his arm, picked up his case and began to walk towards the departure gates.

"So?" She felt like sticking out a foot to trip him up but he was already past, moving too fast, as he always had. "Is that it?"

"Janie," he turned, sweet reason in a suit and tie. "I'll be back in two days—we can talk then." He was gone, neatly side-stepping the bags on the floor, neatly side-stepping her fears.

As he descended the spiral ramp past the conical water feature that was meant to calm passengers, she noticed he had dandruff on the collar of his chalk-stripe suit. Good, she thought.

With the detached observation that airports often bring, she watched other passengers descend. A small Chinese-looking woman with long airbrushed fingernails and an Armani suit seemed too perfect to be real. The flight attendant could probably fold her into a luggage locker and she'd still come out looking immaculate at the other end. Janie had never been like that—she had hair that stuck out and shoes that were scuffed or run over at the back. Would Rob have taken her worries more seriously if she had been better groomed?

Two teenage Australian backpackers chatted down the ramp, tie-dyed t-shirts flapping in synchrony with their mouths. In her gap year, she'd worked in a local crèche. Rob had traveled to Switzerland to study canton politics in his. She wished she'd gone farther, done more.

Another businessman dropping into the depths of the airport—like Rob, but twenty years on. Silver hair, platinum Rolex, red congested features. He was a Type A personality waiting to drop dead. Janie had a sudden vindictive hope he'd do it on Rob's flight. He turned, sketching a wave, and Janie turned too, wondering whom he'd left behind.

She saw the pneumatic cleavage and blonde highlights of a trophy wife—or maybe a mistress—who waved back, but allowed herself a disgusted grimace as soon as the man was out of sight. Right, thought Janie, that's it. If it wasn't an omen, it was at least a warning. She pulled out her mobile and rang the Marie Stopes clinic. "I want a termination," she said clearly, causing heads to turn all across the departure lounge. "In the next two days, if possible. It's…" she paused, wondering how to express her sudden loathing for her life. She looked out at the grey sky, punctuated by clumsy jet airplanes.

"It's convenient timing," she said.

Pushcart-nominated Kay Sexton is an associate editor for Night Train journal. Her work has been a finalist for numerous awards and is widely anthologized. Kay's most recent project, Green Thought in an Urban Shade, was a collaboration with the Irish painter Fion Gunn, to explore and celebrate the parks and urban spaces of Beijing, Dublin, London, and Paris in words and images. Her website is http://www. charybdis.freeserve.co.uk.

THE LOTHARIO

There were enough seats on the tram to Grinzing where the Heligenstadt House was so that Ethan and Giselle found two side by side. The seat facing Ethan was empty, but the one opposite Giselle was occupied by a woman in her sixties who held a small mirror in one hand and a tube of vermilion lipstick in her other. There was a slight indent and pale strip of skin on her left ring finger where a wedding band had dug into her flesh for perhaps forty years. But those years had not slowed her dexterity for applying makeup on a moving vehicle.

Ethan thought there was something odd about a woman of her age and obvious good breeding primping in a public place.

Under her black wool coat, she was dressed in a wine-colored dress and Chantilly lace, the city's splendor echoing in the dress's frill and reserved charm.

Ethan stretched his legs and unconsciously put his feet up on the seat opposite him.

Entfernen Sie Ihre Füße von dem Sitz! the woman snapped at him. He noticed a glint of the future in her still-vibrant blue eyes.

No need to understand German to know what was being said. Giselle watched Ethan remove his feet from the seat and smiled at him. You just got a tongue lashing, she said. I take it you don't need a literal translation?

No, I got the point.

The trolley car creaked and swayed from the people coming on and getting off at the next stop. Although the public transport was on the honor system, people queued up to pay.

Ethan noticed the woman who sat diagonal to him had shifted so that now she looked out the window, making an effort to avoid looking inside the trolley.

An elderly man carrying a small leather briefcase took the seat where Ethan had rested his feet. His hair and groomed handlebar mustache shone the silver of a Gustav Klimt painting.

The Frau opened her hands in her lap. Her palms told nothing of her years. They were fresh and young under a slight layer of perspiration.

Taking a monogrammed handkerchief from her purse, she held it as if waiting for something. Then the tram jerked forward and the hanky fluttered to the floor. Leaning forward, she seemed about to reach for it, but hesitated.

The gray-haired man picked it up, and with a flourish, offered the linen square back to the Frau.

She thanked him with practiced surprise.

Their eyes held. He smiled, tipped his hat deftly, stood, and exited.

Once more the tram started moving.

For a reason Ethan could not surmise, he put his feet back on the gentleman's now vacant seat.

The woman watched him, but this time said nothing as the tram continued on its way.

M. J. Rose is the internationally-bestselling author of eight novels of psychological suspense and two nonfiction books. Her work is published in over twelve countries. She devotes part of her time developing creative marketing solutions for authors and runs the popular blogs, Buzz, Balls & Hype, and Backstory. She can be found online at http://www. mjrose.com.

Robert Reynolds

WHAT YOU CAN LEARN IN A BAR

This German man is telling me about self-defense techniques. His pint has remained untouched at three-quarters full for ten minutes. Make to hit me in the face, he says, pointing to the middle of his glasses. I slowly move my fist toward his nose and he redirects my arm to the side, plants a mock punch to the cheekbone with his other hand. The stool creaks. These are things I teach, he says. I teach for twenty years, off and on. Give me your hand. I hold out my hand and he cradles my thumb between his thumb and forefinger, bounces the hand playfully up and down, taking its weight. To me it seems he has muscles in his fingers. The veins stick out in his forearm, which must be bigger than my biceps. His eyes are small, intense, staring at my hand, staring at me. If you can get hold of the hand, there is much you can do. He twists my arm in a way it shouldn't go and my whole body drifts toward the bar, a brief shock of pain registering in my elbow before he pulls it back. Or the other way. I slide off the stool and have to catch myself with my foot. He doesn't notice me wince, or maybe he does and he doesn't care. It's not about power, he says, it's about knowledge. What is it that he would have me know? Pain, perhaps. Or fear. To know what to do, how to move, he says. Redirect. Make a stabbing motion at my heart. I do what he says and he blocks my arm upward. Two legs of my stool leave the floor. Twenty years I teach this. I ask him, Have you ever been in a situation where you've had to use this? He leans over for his pint, takes a long swallow. Once, years ago. I am at a metro in Hamburg, I walk through a tunnel and two guys come from behind me. One tries to push me down. The other has a knife. I am so surprised I cannot think. They want to steal my bag but I will not let them. All I can do is fight them off, push them away as best I can, keep trying to go forward. I run, I block, push, dodge. He jerks his head one way, makes wild arm movements. I have no control. If I fall down I know they kill me. This goes on for several minutes. Somehow I make it to the end of the tunnel, and I yell. Finally they take off. I make sure that never happen again. He takes another swallow of beer. He nods, as if agreeing with something I've said. He steps off his stool and motions with his hands. Stand up, he says. Now I teach you something, yes?

Robert Reynolds's stories have appeared in Vestal Review, Tampa Review, and at http://www.mrbellersneighborhood.com. He is a former contributing editor and contributing associate, respectively, of the Boston Book Review and the Harvard Review. He is currently working on a collection of stories and a memoir of sorts, called Military Son. He lives in Austin, Texas.

Steve Frederick

LA LUNA DE LOS TRES LIMONES

A cluster of fruit dangled like three moons from the lemon tree outside my balcony. The real moon was nowhere to be seen, obscured by the thatched roof of the hotel, perhaps, or simply too low on the horizon to see.

Brassy mariachi rhythms blared from the town square below, rising fog-like through the turgid tropical air. I lit a Cuban cigar and watched the hips of the cleaning girl sway in time as she swept the stones of the plaza. The watchman had already swung shut the heavy gates, and I pulled the cork on the cheap cane rum I'd secured in the square during the heat of the day.

I had no ice, but with a slice of lemon I could manage to swill the stuff tequila-style. I speared a ripe fruit with my Buck knife and sectioned it neatly into eighths.

I couldn't make out the words, but it was clear the mariachis were yelping a bawdy lyric. The girl stepped livelier in the torchlight, lifting her skirts with one hand and swirling about the flagstones. By the time I finished the first lemon, the rum was seeping through my muscles like a tonic, and I ached to join her.

I plucked a second lemon and sliced it less precisely, then tossed aside the plastic cup and began drinking from the bottle. Deep in the shadows, I was unsure whether the girl was aware that I'd been watching her. If she was, she was being coy about it. She kicked off her sandals and loosened the braid in her hair, letting the knotted end whip at her buttocks. The humid night air and the rum brought beads of sweat to my forehead, and the music filled my veins like a slow-acting hallucinogen. I peeled off my shirt and let the breeze trace feathery hieroglyphs on my chest.

I drew deeply on the cigar, and she suddenly stopped and faced me. She drew a finger to her swollen lips and mocked me, her cheeks sucked inward as if she were drawing me in. I tipped the bottle back and swallowed deeply, grateful that my night had taken a promising turn. The girl laughed loudly and opened her buttons, jiggling her cleavage in my direction. I flicked the cigar butt aside and beckoned to her, and she opened her arms wide.

The music slowed to a dreamy waltz. Out of the shadows below me stepped the watchman, and she floated lightly into his arms. I watched in disbelief as they swayed to the slow, sinuous rhythm, both oblivious to the deluded fool in the shadows above.

I plucked the third lemon and hurled it hard over the wall. A chattered curse answered from the street below, giving the lovers pause for a brief, distracted moment.

Steve Frederick is a Nebraska writer. This story was his first work of very short fiction.

Bruce Holland Rogers

HOW COULD A MOTHER?

It's better doing this woman to woman, don't you think?

Before we get started, is there anything you need? Do you want something to drink? Coffee? A soft drink? Do you need to use the bathroom?

How had the day gone, before all this started? Were you at home the entire day, both you and your boyfriend? Had your boyfriend been drinking? Had you been drinking? How much did he drink during the day? In the evening? And you? How much did you have? Can you estimate? More than a six-pack? More than two six-packs? Was your daughter in the house with you the whole time?

When was it that your daughter—when was it that Josie started to cry? What was your state of mind when you punished her? What were you thinking when she wouldn't stop crying? Did your boyfriend say anything about Josie's crying? What did he say? What did you do to make her stop? Then, what did your boyfriend do? Did you do anything to restrain him? Did you say anything? No, I mean, did you say anything to your boyfriend about what he was doing to your daughter?

Did you try to wake her up right away? Did you check her pulse? Did you listen for her breathing? When was the next time that you checked on her condition?

What time did you wake up? How soon after you woke up did you check on your daughter? You could tell right away? How did you know? Then what did you do? Was the abduction story his idea, or yours? Which car did you take? How did you come to choose Cascadia State Park? Had you been to the area before? When had he been there? Did he say anything to you about why he thought the park would be a good place? Where were you when you called the police to report her missing?

Is there anything you'd like to add?

Does this typescript accurately reflect what you have told me? Do you need more time to read it before you sign?

Can you guess how it feels for me, even with all the practice I have, to ask these questions? Do you wonder what questions I'm not able to ask you? Do you wonder if I have children of my own? Are you a monster? What is a monster? Did you know there were officers like me who handled only cases like this, one after another? Do you have any thoughts about the question no one can answer? Not the one everyone asks, but the one only a mother who has felt her own hands shake with a rage that is bigger than she is can ask? Not that I'd willingly trade the suffering on my side of the table for the suffering on your side, but why haven't I? Why not?

Bruce Holland Rogers is the author of four collections of stories, and is especially known for writing very, very short fiction. Readers all over the world receive his stories by e-mail subscription from http://www. shortshortshort.com. He lives in Eugene, Oregon.

Tom Hazuka

UTILITARIANISM

I return home for the first time as an adult. My parents greet me traditionally, Mom worrying "that woman" isn't feeding me enough, Dad crushing my hand lest I forget which one of us survived Guadalcanal. But an odor of arrested decay has replaced the smells of childhood. The house of my youth is decorated with death.

Stuffed creatures fill the rooms. Local varmints predominate—squirrels, chipmunks, some possums and porcupines, even a bullfrog—but Dad hangs my coat on an eight-point buck, and the TV blares from the belly of a rampant and silently roaring grizzly. We stand entranced, almost touching.

"I bet you could eat a horse," Mom says, and bustles to the kitchen.

"You know Jeremy Bentham, the philosopher?" Dad asks. "*He's* stuffed. Mom and I are going to London to see him."

My father has hardly left the state since World War II.

"Your favorite! Liverwurst on rye."

Mom puts the sandwich and a glass of milk on the dining room table. Then I see that the cat I grew up with is the centerpiece.

"You embalmed Kitten!"

"Embalming is for graveyards, son. Mom and I fixed Kitten to be with us forever."

I can't eat with a corpse staring at me. "Where did you get all these, these *dead* things?"

"My God, boy," Mom says. "Open your eyes." A shadow nicks her face. "I thought you loved liverwurst."

"Your mother saw the ad in the magazine," Dad says, the two of them beaming as he puts his arm around her for the first time in my memory.

Tom Hazuka is a professor of English at Central Connecticut State University. He has published two novels, The Road to the Island and In the City of the Disappeared, and one book of nonfiction, A Method to March Madness: An Insider's Look at the Final Four (co-written with C.J. Jones). His young adult novel, Last Chance for First, will be published in 2008. He has co-edited three other short story anthologies: A Celestial Omnibus: Short Fiction on Faith (Beacon Press); Flash Fiction (W.W. Norton); and Best American Flash Fiction of the 21st Century (Shanghai Foreign Language Education Press). His short fiction, essays, and poems have appeared in many literary magazines.

Bruce Holland Rogers

THREE SOLDIERS

1. The Hardest Question

My marines bring me questions. "When do we get to shower?" "Sergeant, how do you say 'Good afternoon' again?" "Sarge, where can I get more gun oil?"

I have answers. "Tomorrow, maybe." *"Maysuh alheer."* "Use mine."

Answering their questions is my job. But when Anaya was shot and bleeding out, he grabbed my arm and said, "Sergeant? Sergeant?" I understood the question, but damn. I didn't have an answer.

2. Foreign War

No U.S. soldier who could see that kid would have shot him. But that's long-range ordnance for you. Calder stood next to me in the street, looking at the pieces. "We've come so far from home," he said, "that we'll never get back."

"You dumbass," I said. But a year later, I stood on the tarmac hugging my child, thinking of that kid in pieces, and I wasn't home.

3. Decisions, Decisions

In morning twilight far away, my men are making up their minds:

What's that guy carrying?

Friend or foe?

I should be there, helping them decide. My wife and my parents do their best to make Christmas dinner conversation around my silence. An hour ago, I was yelling at Angie for turning on the damn news. My father, carving, won't meet my eyes. He says, "White meat, or dark?"

Bruce Holland Rogers is the author of four collections of stories, and is especially known for writing very, very short fiction. Readers all over the world receive his stories by e-mail subscription from http://www. shortshortshort.com. He lives in Eugene, Oregon.

SKIN DEEP

Claude returns from the coffee house to find his suitcase splayed across the motel bed and the manager's wife picking through his shirts and underwear.

"Is this a scam?" He sets the cup of bitter coffee on the television. "Your husband sends me across the street while you rip me off?"

She shakes her head. "Nothing that fancy." Crossing her arms, she grips her shoulders: white blouse, frayed jeans, bare feet. A decade younger than her husband and as thin as a prayer. "Wondered what I could tell about you from your things." Her tongue lingers in the dark aperture between the rows of teeth. The face she shows him is narrow, pale, lovely. "Don't tell Teddy. He has a temper." Not long ago she shaved her head, the down a filter through which she must be seen. "I haven't taken anything." She extends her arms, standing cruciform. "Search me."

"Not necessary," Claude says.

"Frisk me."

"Forget it."

"You'll feel better if you're certain." Then she adds, "Close the door first."

"I don't need to search you." He closes the door.

"I'll shut my eyes."

Her clothing is tight, her bones the bones of a bird. She couldn't hide a matchbook. Claude runs his hands along her ribs and down her thighs. She remains in the windmill position. He pats against her back and buttocks. He presses against her small breasts. Finally he pushes her arms down, which causes her eyes to open, as if she were a mechanical doll.

"Satisfied?" she asks.

"What does my bag tell you about me?"

"You dress well. And you don't know yourself."

"I forgot to check here." He slips a finger inside the waist of her jeans, the gap between the denim and her pale skin. He paces a circle around her, rimming her pants with his finger. When he stands in front of her again, he lifts her shirt: small breasts, nipples upturned, fruit plucked prematurely from the vine.

"I guess you're clean," he says.

"Certain?"

He unbuttons her jeans, tugs them down. Her panties slide along her thighs, slanting and rippled like a flag. Her pubis is shaved to a narrow strip. His hand slides between her legs.

"You don't appear to be hiding anything."

She grips his hand and begins rocking her pelvis. "I can come like this." A drop of sweat forms beneath her fine hair, the scalp turning pink.

After, she says, "Watch me walk." She shuffles with her pants down to the bathroom. "You have to do yourself," she calls. "I'm a married woman." Her laughter's round, complicated, lovely to hear. She reappears, buttoning the jeans. "We have rules about what I should and shouldn't do."

"You should gain some weight," Claude says.

A veil descends. "I like myself this way." She slams the door twice before the latch clicks.

Claude slides the chain into its slot. He takes the paper cup from the television, the coffee still warm, still bitter and burnt, but easier to swallow.

Robert Boswell is the author of five novels, Century's Son, American Owned Love, Mystery Ride, The Geography of Desire, and Crooked Hearts; two story collections, Living to Be 100, and Dancing in the Movies; and one play, Tongues. His stories have appeared in Esquire, the New Yorker, Best American Short Stories, O. Henry Prize Stories, Pushcart Prize, and elsewhere. Robert shares the Cullen Chair in Creative Writing at the University of Houston with his wife, Antonya Nelson.

No Questions Asked

I'd had less than twenty bucks in it, and I'd cancelled the credit cards when I noticed it was gone. But it was a nice wallet, and I sorely missed the personal mementos—a few photos, a half-dollar that had always brought me luck, a particularly apt fortune cookie fortune. So I took out the ad:

"Lost Wallet—blk men's, l/s city library. Rwd if Ret—No Questions Asked."

One week later, I got the call.

"Are you certain?" A raspy voice, slow, stumbling, as though repeating syllables learned by rote.

"Absolutely. Twenty bucks, no questions."

"You swear to that? Promise, and I will come."

I did.

He was good as his word, the gangly, hunched-over man in the baggy brown coat. We met in the park. His eyes burned with a bloodshot ferocity. His gloved fingers thrust it upon me as though it burned him. He never spoke.

Now my wallet glows under ultraviolet light. Sometimes I see scales in the pattern of the black leather, or perhaps they are circles. At times, it suddenly burns, heavy with scorching urgency. Other times it is cold, afraid, burrowing into the recess of my pocket. Each time, I spin and search the crowd in the street around me, looking for a reason, a logic. I find nothing.

The fortune cookie fortune is subtly altered, the meaning different though the words are unchanged. The lucky numbers on the back now form the Fibonacci sequence. My lucky half-dollar shows the leering countenance of a man I do not recognize.

I cannot throw it away. I have tried, but always I must return, sifting frantically through the dumpster until my fingers bleed, until I find it. I put it in a lead-lined box when I go to sleep to avoid unnatural dreams, filled with words in a language I do not understand, though I have learned the syllables by rote.

I see him, the man in the baggy brown coat. I see him in the street, the subway, the library from time to time. He smiles at me, a rictus grin, and I glare or shudder as my pocket burns, grows heavy.

But I never ask.

After all, a promise is a promise.

Patrick Weekes has published stories in Amazing Stories, Realms of Fantasy, Strange Horizons, and several anthologies and small-press magazines. He currently lives with his wife and son in Canada, where he writes video games by day and novels by night.

It's easier to resist at the
beginning than at the end.

MARK BUDMAN

Mark Budman has always been interested in short-shorts. To him, a short-short is not only a stepping stone to writing longer fiction, but a drawing power that could bring the busy masses back to literature. With his co-editor Sue O'Neill, he started *Vestal Review*, a magazine of flash fiction, back in March of 2000. Together with Sue, he has published thirty quarterly issues so far.

Mark has been lecturing widely on the subject of flash. He taught it at Binghamton University, Ithaca College, Broome Community College, Art School Online, and is scheduled to be a panelist for the Saltonstall Foundation.

Mark was born and raised in the former Soviet Union, but now resides in New York state. His novel *My Life at First Try* was scheduled for publication in May of 2008 by Counterpoint.

TOM HAZUKA

Tom Hazuka graduated from Fairfield University, and spent 1978-80 with the Peace Corps in Chile. He received a MA in English/creative writing from the University of California at Davis and a PhD from the University of Utah, and is currently a professor of English at Central Connecticut State University.

His first novel, *The Road to the Island*, is set in Connecticut; another novel, *In the City of the Disappeared*, takes place in Chile during the Pinochet dictatorship. He has recently completed a young adult novel, *Last Chance for First*. His latest book is *A Method to March Madness: An Insider's Look at the Final Four*, written with CCSU Athletics Director C.J. Jones. Among more than thirty published stories, "Carnivores" won the Snake Nation Review Fiction Competition, "Vaporware" and "Headless Angel" were finalists in the Sun Dog World's Best Short Short Story Competition, and "All She Wrote" and "Purchase Virgins" were nominated for a Pushcart Prize. He has received the Bruce P. Rossley Award for New England Writers, a State of Connecticut Artist Fellowship, and has been a Bread Loaf Scholar at the Bread Loaf Writers' Conference.

A former co-editor of *Quarterly West* magazine, Hazuka has also co-edited two popular short story anthologies: *A Celestial Omnibus: Short Fiction on Faith* (Beacon Press, 1997), and *Flash Fiction* (W.W. Norton, 1992). A third anthology, *Best American Flash Fiction of the 21st Century*, was published in China (Shanghai Foreign Language Education Press, 2007).

Ooligan Press

CREDITS

Ooligan Press takes its name from a Native American word for the common smelt or candlefish. Ooligan is a general trade press rooted in the rich literary life of Portland and the Department of English at Portland State University. The press is staffed by students pursuing masters degrees in an apprenticeship program under the guidance of a core faculty of publishing professionals.

Lead Editor
Laura Howe

Lead Designer
Terra Chapek

Proofreaders
Emilee Newman Bowles
Kari Smit
Kate Willms

Lead Publicist
Liz Fuller

The following Ooligan Press students also contributed to the making of *You Have Time for This*:

Editing: Katrina Hill, Aquisitions Workgroup Manager; Joanna Schmidt, Editing Workgroup Manager; Karen Brattain; Dana Clark; Rebecca Daniels; Jennifer Davis; Jay Evans; Rosalie Grafem; Haili Graff; Angela Hodge; Ryan Hume; Anthony Jackson; Bo Johnson; Jake Keszler; Paulette Rees-Denis; Irene Ridgway; and Ruth Scovill.

Design: Abbey Gaterud, Design Workgroup Manager; and Alan Dubinsky.

Marketing: Sara Freedman, Mike Hirte, Robert Elee Jackson, Jake Keszler, Miala Leong, Erin Malus, and Laura Meehan.

Colophon

Interior title: 41 pt Futura Std Heavy
Interior type: 10.5 pt Adobe Garamond Pro Regular
Authors' names: 18 pt Optima LT Std Bold Italic
Story titles: 16 pt Optima LT Std Roman
Photographs: Casey Rae Wickum
Paper: 60# white

Ordering Information

Ooligan Press titles are distributed to the book trade by Graphic Arts Center Publishing Company (www.gacpc.com) and are available at all major national and regional wholesalers. For ordering information please call 800.452.3032 or use the instructions from the Graphic Arts Center catalog. To request a catalog please phone 800.84.BOOKS.

Our books also may be purchased directly from the press by phone, fax, post, or email. Educators, please contact us for a special discount on classroom sets.

Ooligan Press
PO Box 751
Portland, OR 97207-0751
www.ooliganpress.pdx.edu
503.725.9410
ooligan@pdx.edu